What will Emily's future hold?

At the campfire, Marie clapped her hands to get everyone's attention, then announced, "Foals, Fillies, and Thoros, it is my pleasure and privilege to inform you that, tonight, Webster's Country Horse Camp has been honored by a visit from a very special person. Ladies and gentlemen, please welcome that celebrated mind reader, mystic, and medium, *Madame Beatrice*!"

Everybody whistled, cheered, and clapped as a wiry little gypsy stepped out of the shadows. She was dressed in a bright yellow blouse and a red print skirt with a long fringed sash of purple and blue around her waist. A red-and-white bandanna was tied around her head, and gold hoop earrings dangled from her ears.

Her fingers felt cool and dry as she took Emily's hand and peered closely at the palm. "Ahhh . . . I see that you vill discover a treasure—a treasure of pure gold!"

Emily stared at her. "A treasure? Pure gold?" That didn't make any sense at all.

As the group began a camp song, an image began to form in Emily's mind. Suddenly she leaped to her feet. "I got it!" she shouted. "My costume! For the Costume Parade!"

The gypsy smiled and said, "I told you y[o]u would."

Other books in the **HORSE CRAZY** series:

GOOD SPORTS

by Virginia Vail

Illustrated by Daniel Bodé

Troll Associates

Library of Congress Cataloging-in-Publication Data

Vail, Virginia.
    Good sports / by Virginia Vail; illustrated by Daniel Bode.
        p.   cm.—(Horse crazy ; #3)
    Summary: The girls at Webster's Country Horse Camp despair of
winning the upcoming sports and riding competition with a rival
boys' camp, until Libby's unconventional grandmother shows up to
coach them in softball.
    ISBN 0-8167-1629-3 (lib. bdg.)   ISBN 0-8167-1630-7 (pbk.)
    [1. Camps—Fiction.   2. Softball—Fiction.   3. Grandmothers—
Fiction.   4. Horses—Fiction.]   I. Bode, Daniel, ill.   II. Title.
III. Series: Vail, Virginia.   Horse crazy ; #3.
PZ7.V192Go   1990
[Fic]—dc19   89-31345

A TROLL BOOK, published by Troll Associates,
Mahwah, NJ 07430

10   9   8   7   6   5   4   3   2   1

Chapter One

Dear Judy,

I know, I know—I promised I'd write to you every single day to tell you everything that's happening here at Webster's, but so much has been happening lately that this is the very first chance I've had to get caught up. I can hardly believe I've been here two whole weeks already! Time flies when you're having fun!

Emily Jordan paused for a minute, reading over what she'd just written. Considering that her best friend, Judy Bradford, was sitting at home with her leg in a cast instead of sharing this summer at Webster's Country Horse Camp, maybe it wasn't very nice to mention how the time was flying for Emily. For Judy, these two weeks probably seemed more like two years. Emily thought about starting a new letter on a fresh sheet of paper, but decided against it. She had so much to tell Judy that if she didn't keep going, the rest of her cabin mates would come back, and then she'd never be able to finish.

The Fillies' cabin was quiet now, deserted except for Emily, so she could concentrate on her letter. Libby, the sparkly little redhead who wanted to be a jockey, had taken Dru and her friend Penny down to the sheep pasture to play with the lambs. Danny and Lynda were sunbathing down on the dock by the Winnepac River, and Caro had gone off somewhere with her Thoroughbred friends. The Thoros were the oldest campers at Webster's, girls aged fifteen and sixteen, and Caro preferred to hang out with them though she was only fourteen, one year older than Emily. That was okay with the rest of the Fillies—"Princess Caroline" was a real pain in the neck most of the time.

You remember Dru, the Filly I told you about who's kind of overweight and miserable all the time? Well, last week after our overnight trail ride that turned into a disaster because she fell off her horse, Dru disappeared! *I mean, she just* vanished! *We were all really worried about her, and everybody was looking all over for her, and guess who finally found her? Me! She'd run away, or she started to run away, and then she changed her mind and hid in an empty stall in the barn. I tripped over her when I went to get a rag to rub down Joker after I took him out without permission to search for her. We all tried to help her feel good about herself, so now she's not scared of horses anymore—or at least, not as much—and she*

2

actually won a special prize for Most Improved Rider in our first horse show. Isn't that neat???

Next Sunday is the big Field Day with Long Branch, the boys' camp on the other side of the river. Remember what it said in the brochure about Field Day? That's when the boys come here and compete against Webster's girls in volleyball, softball, swimming, boating, and horsemanship, and there's a barbecue afterwards. Libby and Lynda say that the boys usually win at absolutely everything *except horsemanship, and I guess they know what they're talking about because they've been coming here for years. The boys will probably win again this year, because the only thing we're really good at is riding. But when it comes to horsemanship and mounted games, those Long Branch boys don't stand a chance!*

The most exciting thing about Field Day is the Costume Parade. The boys think it's silly, and they don't dress up, so the competition is just among the campers at Webster's, but the boys like to watch. We all have to make our own costumes out of stuff we find ourselves. Marie has a huge box that her new refrigerator came in, and it's filled with odds and ends of fabric and old clothes and other things she's collected that we're allowed to use. What's driving me crazy is that I don't know what to be. We're supposed to costume our horses, too, and I just can't think of anything wonderful *enough for Joker.*

Thinking about the big palomino she'd been assigned for the summer, Emily put down her pen and stared dreamily into space. Joker deserved the very best of everything, and that included the very best costume Emily could imagine. But so far she hadn't come up with any ideas, and time was running out.

A mosquito whined close to Emily's ear, and she swatted at it. She missed the mosquito, but hit her ear so hard that it brought tears to her eyes. It also brought her attention back to her letter.

If you were here I bet you'd have the most fantastic costume of all. You're so good at things like that. You're really creative, and I'm not. I guess if worse comes to worst, I could go as Lady Godiva. Then I wouldn't have to wear any costume at all! I don't think Matt and Marie would approve, though! And since they own and run the camp, I guess maybe I'd better try to think of something else.

Did I already tell you how neat our counselor, Pam Webster, is? She loves her job because she likes people almost as much as she likes horses! All of the Websters love horses. Matt used to ride champion jumpers on the show circuit, you know, and Marie's a good rider, too. And boy, is she a great cook! If I didn't ride so much, and swim, and stuff like that, I'd turn into a blimp by the end of the summer! And it's so much fun, helping her prepare our meals.

Emily smiled, remembering how she'd almost decided not to come to camp at all because of Judy's accident. She and Judy had always done everything together, and Emily had been afraid she'd be lonely and homesick without her best friend. Well, she'd been a little homesick at first, but not for long. And as for being lonely, that just wasn't possible because of

Libby, Lynda, Danny, Penny, and Dru. Caro, too, of course, except that Caro was awfully hard to like.

In spite of Caro, Emily was really glad she'd come to Webster's after all. Next summer, she and Judy would be Fillies together. They'd have riding lessons every day, care for their horses, do chores around the farm, go on hayrides and cookouts and trail rides, and do all the wonderful things Emily was doing this summer.

"I wonder if Joker will remember me when I come back?" Emily said aloud. She looked at the photograph she'd taken of the palomino—she'd taped it up on the wall over her bunk, right next to a photo of her mother, her father, and her older brother, Eric. Emily knew she'd never, ever forget Joker, but she also knew that nine months was a very long time, especially for a horse. No, she decided with a sigh, he probably wouldn't remember her. She'd just have to remind him who she was, that's all. She knew it was silly, but she couldn't help feeling a little sad.

"Wow, is it ever *hot* out there!" Lynda Graves gasped as she and Danny Franciscus burst into the cabin. "I was being broiled alive! You were smart to stay inside, Emily. Finish that letter yet?"

"Almost," Emily said. "I was just telling Judy about the Costume Parade and Field Day."

"Have you decided what your costume's going to be?" Danny asked, plopping herself down on the foot of Emily's bunk.

"No—I can't make up my mind, and it's driving me

crazy." Emily put down her pad of stationery and her pen. "What about you? What're you going to be?"

"I don't know, either," Danny admitted, lifting her mane of thick, dark hair off her neck with one hand and fanning herself with the other. "Whew! It's not any cooler in here than it is outside. Lynda, how about turning on that fan?"

Lynda, who had just come out of the bathroom where she'd splashed cold water on her face and neck, paused to flick the switch on the electric fan that was perched on one of the windowsills. Then she pulled down one of the straps of her bright blue tank suit and groaned at the contrast between the pale skin underneath and her rosy shoulders and arms.

"Look at that, will you? Serves me right for not putting on enough sunscreen."

"Does it hurt?" Emily asked. "I have some aloe stuff my mom gave me. It's kind of green and slimy, but it takes the sting out, and you won't peel."

"I'll try anything," Lynda said. "I don't care how slimy it is as long as I don't peel."

Emily hopped off her bunk and rummaged in her camp trunk, finally coming up with a plastic squeeze bottle which she tossed to Lynda.

Lynda immediately began rubbing the green gel onto her arms and chest. "Thanks, Emily. Funny— back home in Iowa I never get sunburned. Guess that's because, working on the farm, I'm always all covered up." She darted a glance at Danny. "But *you're* as brown as an Indian. I bet you never peel."

6

Danny grinned. "I thought Indians were supposed to be redskins!" She stretched out one slim, tanned leg. "I am pretty dark, aren't I? You're right—I never burn. But then, I always remember to baste myself with tanning lotion."

"Hey, Danny, that's it!" Emily cried.

"What's it?" Danny asked, puzzled.

"An Indian! An Indian princess! That's what your costume should be! Wouldn't she make a great Indian princess, Lynda?"

"Oh, yeah! Terrific!" Lynda agreed. "Danny, you could be Pocahontas or somebody. And you can ride Misty bareback, the way the Indians do!"

Danny's big, dark eyes lit up. "An Indian princess . . . Hey, that really *is* a terrific idea! Let's see— we're in Mohawk country. Maybe I could be a Mohawk princess, with a wampum necklace, and feathers in my hair, and braids. . . . Fabulous! I'll be the last of the Mohawks!"

She began quickly braiding her hair and fastened the ends with two of Penny's rubber bands. Then she walked over to the dresser next to Caro's bunk and picked up one of Caro's hair ribbons and tied it around her head.

"Here, Danny, use my pheasant feather," Lynda suggested, handing her a long, graceful quill. "I found it on the lawn the other day."

Danny stuck the feather into her headband and smiled at her reflection in the mirror. "Look—instant Indian!"

"What's your costume going to be, Lynda?" Emily asked.

"I'm going to be a knight in shining armor," Lynda said promptly. "All I need is a couple miles of aluminum foil. I'll wrap myself up in it . . ."

"Like a baked potato?" Danny said, giggling.

Lynda gave her a mock scowl. "*Not* like a baked potato, though I guess if it's as hot as this on Sunday I'll probably roast. I already have a helmet—Marie gave me one of those plastic gallon bottles of apple cider—without the cider, that is. I'm going to cut off the bottom and make a hole for my face, and cover the whole thing with foil."

"Sounds great as long as nobody tosses you on the grill!" Emily teased.

Lynda laughed. "I hadn't thought that I might be mistaken for part of the picnic, not part of the parade. I'll wear a sign that says DO NOT COOK!"

They all cracked up. Emily was glad that Lynda and Danny had decided on their costumes, but she still hadn't come up with a good idea for her own, and there wasn't much time—Field Day was less than a week away. What about Robin Hood? Or Maid Marian? That wasn't very exciting. Joan of Arc? No, Lynda was going to be wearing armor. A cowgirl? Too trite. A jester or a clown? No, that wasn't Emily's style—too babyish. A Canadian Mountie? Not bad, but not very original, either.

Emily sighed and scribbled the closing to her letter:

9

Lynda and Danny just came in. Lynda's going to be a knight for the costume parade and Danny's going to be an Indian princess, but I still don't know what I'm going to be. When I find out, I'll write. Gotta run now—I want to catch the mailman, and he usually shows up just about now. I'll keep you posted!

Love, Emily

She was just about to fold the letter when she realized that she hadn't once asked how Judy was feeling. Quickly she added a P.S.: *How's your leg? I bet you're getting real good at using crutches. But don't do anything dumb and break your other leg! (Just kidding!)*

Now Emily stuck the letter in an envelope, addressed and stamped it, then pulled on a pair of shorts over her bathing suit and slipped her feet into her rubber thong sandals.

"I'm going up to the mailbox. Anybody want to come along?" she asked.

"Why not?" Lynda said. "Maybe we can scare up a real breeze on the way. All this fan is doing is moving the hot air around." She, too, had pulled on shorts over her tank suit, and was lacing up her high-top sneakers. "Then we can go straight down to the river for water sports."

"Not just water sports," Danny reminded her, unbraiding her hair and returning the rubber bands, ribbon, and feather. "Volleyball and softball, too. We have to practice like crazy for the game on Sunday. Better put on your sneakers, Emily."

"Right—I almost forgot."

10

Emily sat back down, took off her sandals, and started putting on socks and sneakers. "It's us against the Thoros today, isn't it? And Rachel's coaching." Rachel Orbison was the Thoros' counselor, and the camp's volleyball and softball coach. Rachel had told the Fillies and Thoros that this whole week was going to be devoted to brushing up on their game. Melinda Willis, the Foals' counselor, was in charge of swimming and boating, and she'd agreed that it was more important for the older girls to give up water sports for a few days and concentrate on softball and volleyball. For the rest of the week, Melinda would be coaching the Foals in swimming—they at least had a chance against the younger Long Branch campers.

"This is going to be some week!" Danny added. "What with all this practice, not to mention working every spare minute on horsemanship and mounted games, and making our costumes, we'll all be *dead* on Sunday! I feel like we're in training for the Olympics or something!"

Lynda grinned. "We are—the Winnepac Camp Olympics! Webster's girls have been competing against Long Branch boys for years. Matt and Marie believe there's no reason girls shouldn't be as good at sports as boys. And that means *all* sports, not just riding. It would be so *neat* if we could beat them at volleyball and softball. We never have."

"If you want *my* opinion, *I* think the whole idea is absolutely ridiculous!"

Caro Lescaux, sleek and sassy in fashionable shorts,

11

T-shirt, and sandals, a pair of designer sunglasses perched atop her golden head, stepped into the cabin. She strode over to her bunk and tossed a shopping bag onto it. Emily recognized the name on the bag. It came from the only fancy boutique in the town of Winnepac, and probably contained yet another piece of expensive clothing to add to Caro's already impressive wardrobe.

"I don't remember asking for your opinion, Caro," Lynda said casually. "But now that you've given it, *why* do you think it's ridiculous?"

"Because girls and boys are *different*," Caro said. She began to strip off her clothes, tossing them on the floor, and rummaged in her glossy new camp trunk for one of her many bathing suits.

No kidding, Emily thought but didn't say.

"No kidding!" Lynda said aloud. "Believe it or not, Caro, you're not the first person who's noticed that."

Emily stifled a giggle. Lynda might be what Caro would consider a hick—a farm girl from Iowa—but Lynda definitely wasn't cowed by Caro's sophistication.

Caro arched her perfect brows as she fastened the top of her bikini. "What I *mean* is, girls shouldn't compete with boys. If they do, they'll *never* get any dates."

"Dates aren't where it's at," Lynda said. "Webster's girls don't *date* Long Branch boys. Webster's isn't a matchmaking service."

Caro wiggled into her bikini bottom. "That's for sure!"

12

"Don't forget your sneakers, Caro," Emily put in. "Volleyball, remember?"

"Volleyball!" Caro heaved a gusty sigh. "Surely you must all know by now that sports just aren't my thing. This whole Field Day nonsense makes me positively ill. I don't know one end of a volleyball from the other."

"Volleyballs don't have ends," Danny said sweetly. "They're *round*. You hit them into the air over a net."

"Hey, guys, I really want to mail this letter," Emily said to Danny and Lynda. "Are you coming with me or not?"

"We're coming, we're coming," Lynda said.

"Volleyball!" Caro muttered. "And softball's even worse. Softballs are *hard*! If you catch one, you could break a fingernail!" She admired her own long nails. "Come to think of it, I really need a manicure. I bought some new polish this afternoon—it's called Pink Poison. I'll do my toes, too—there's plenty of time before water sports."

"And volleyball," Lynda reminded her, heading for the door.

Caro made a face. "As if I could forget!"

"What else did you buy in town, Caro?" Danny asked, as Emily and Lynda waited impatiently in the doorway.

"Oh, just a few odds and ends. Here, I'll show you." Caro picked up the shopping bag and dumped its contents on her bunk. "Aren't these adorable?" she said, holding up a skirt in a bright tropical print and a tur-

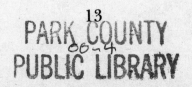

quoise cotton top. "They were a terrific bargain—twenty-five dollars for the skirt, marked down from twenty-seven fifty, and only fifteen for the top. The top wasn't on sale, but it's a Jimmy Jo Original, and I saw the very same thing in a magazine for nineteen ninety-nine. And then I got four pairs of socks—turquoise, peach, banana, and tangerine."

"Sounds like you went grocery shopping rather than buying clothes," Lynda said with a grin. "Speaking of clothes, what's your costume going to be for the parade on Sunday?"

Caro smiled mysteriously. "That's for me to know and you to find out. It's going to be a surprise, but I'll tell you one thing. You're all going to be *green* with envy when you see it!"

Emily sighed. "I'll bet. Listen, I really have to go or I'm going to miss the mailman."

"Oh, yes—the mailman. If he comes while you're there, see if there's a package for me, will you? A *big* package," Caro said. "And if it comes, would you do me a huge favor and bring it back to the cabin?"

"Sure," Emily said, though she wasn't too crazy about the idea of doing a favor for Caro. "Coming, Lynda, Danny?"

The three girls trooped out of the bunkhouse, leaving Caro to her Pink Poison and her new purchases.

"I wonder what's in that package Caro's expecting?" Danny said.

"Probably more clothes—the poor girl doesn't have a *thing* to wear," Lynda replied.

Laughing, Emily said, "Yeah, I really feel sorry for Caro. It must be rough to be so underprivileged. Race you to the mailbox!"

Chapter Two

The flag was still up on the mailbox by the road in front of the Websters' farmhouse, so Emily knew the mailman hadn't come yet. She shoved her letter in among the other campers' letters and postcards and peered down the road, but there was no sign of the mailman's blue and white truck. Well, she wasn't going to wait around—if Caro's package arrived, somebody would be sure to see that she received it.

Just then Libby Dexter, Penny Marshall, and Dru Carpenter came charging up to Emily, Lynda, and Danny.

"You all ready for volleyball practice?" Libby said breathlessly. "We just saw Rachel, and she says softball practice is going to be tonight right after supper, so it's just volleyball this afternoon. She's not feeling so good, but she says she'll be okay tonight. This is the year we're gonna *cream* those Long Branch boys!"

"Yeah, we're gonna *cream* them!" Penny echoed. Her usually calm face was pink and smiling, framed by neat blond braids.

"I petted a lamb," Dru said softly. "It was so little and cute. I don't know if it was a boy or a girl, but I called it Daisy, so I hope it's a girl." Dru looked happy, too, Emily noticed. Winning the award for Most Improved Rider had made a big difference in Dru's personality. Instead of being sorrowful, frightened, and silent all the time, the plump girl had perked up a lot. She didn't even seem to mind that her braces caught the light and sparkled when she smiled.

"Where's Caro?" Libby asked.

"Back at the cabin," Emily said. "I don't think she's going to be an asset when we play against the Long Branch boys. Caro doesn't believe in girls competing against boys."

"Caro doesn't believe it's worth breaking a fingernail to score in softball," Lynda added drily.

Libby shrugged. "Like my grandmother says, it takes all kinds. Maybe Caro will distract the boys' attention so they don't notice if we're safe or out!"

The girls began to walk in the direction of the Winnepac River. Birds chirped and twittered overhead in the branches of the tall, old trees, and the scent of fresh-cut grass was all around them. In the distance, Emily could hear the muted roar of the mower as Chris or Warren Webster piloted it across the fields.

"Do the counselors compete on Field Day?" Danny asked. "Or is it just the campers?"

17

"Only the campers," Lynda said. "The counselors just coach and stuff like that. It works out pretty well, because Long Branch is a small camp like Webster's— they never have more than twenty-five boys. We've got Foals, Fillies, and Thoros, and they have Juniors, Intermediates, and Seniors. We're pretty evenly matched."

"But Webster's is a *horse* camp, and Long Branch is just a camp," Libby put in. "That's why we almost always win the horsemanship competitions and the mounted games."

"I think the mounted games are going to be the most fun," Penny said. "I wish we had more time to practice, though."

"We'll have plenty of time," Lynda said. "For the rest of the week we'll all be practicing during every riding class, and each afternoon, too."

"I hope I don't fall off," Dru said, looking worried. Then she brightened. "I know what I'm going to be for the costume parade, though. I'm going to be the Wicked Witch from *The Wizard of Oz*. Marie says she has an old black dress I can wear, and I'm going to make a black, pointy hat and long, stringy hair out of crepe paper or something. Donna's going to be a Flying Monkey." Donna was the plump little strawberry roan mare that had been assigned to Dru for the summer.

"*Donna?* A Flying Monkey?" Libby echoed. "How're you going to manage that?"

18

Dru shrugged. "I'm not quite sure yet, but Rachel said she'll help me. She has lots of good ideas."

"I'm going to be a bareback rider, like in the circus," Penny said eagerly. "Marie told me she has a tutu that Pam wore in a ballet recital when she was around my age and she's sure it'll fit me. She says it's pink, with lots of sequins."

Danny's eyes widened. "Pam used to take *ballet?*"

Emily couldn't help giggling. She just couldn't picture their tall, rangy counselor flitting across a stage in pink sequins. Pam just wasn't the tutu type!

Libby picked up a pine cone and tossed it in the air. "My grandmother used to be a bareback rider in a circus," she said. "That was way back in the forties, when she was young. She had red hair, like mine, and she rode a white horse named Snowflake."

"Wow!" Emily whispered, impressed. Libby had mentioned that her grandparents had brought her up after her parents had died, but she had never said anything about her grandmother being a circus performer.

"That's fantastic, Libby!" Dru said. "I didn't think grandmothers ever did things like that!"

Libby grinned. "Well, she wasn't a grandmother then! My granddad saw her in the circus when he was home on leave from the army, and he fell in love with her at first sight. They got married right away."

"That's the most romantic thing I ever heard," Danny sighed. "Did she keep it up after they were married?"

"Oh, no," Libby said. "The circus—it was only a *little* circus—went out of business, and Gram settled down with Granddad after the war. But she didn't settle down *too* much," she added with an impish grin. "In her spare time, she exercised racehorses. Guess that's why I'm so horse crazy. And that's why I'm going to be a jockey for the Costume Parade. I just wish we could have a race on Field Day! I bet Foxy could outrun any of the Long Branch horses."

Emily walked along, frowning a little. Libby was going to be a jockey, Dru was going to be a wicked witch, Penny was going to be a bareback rider, Danny was going to be an Indian princess, and Lynda was going to be a knight in shining armor. That left Emily and Caro. And Caro had a secret plan for her costume. Emily was the only Filly who hadn't made up her mind. If she didn't decide soon, she'd probably end up as a bag lady, wearing all the odds and ends that were left over in Marie's refrigerator box!

"Hey, Melinda's on the lifeguard stand!" Lynda cried. "Terrific! C'mon, gang—let's take a dip before we start volleyball practice!"

After the Fillies, Foals, and Thoros had their swim, the older girls trotted over to the volleyball net for practice. Rachel was there waiting for them, a whistle around her neck and the volleyball in her hands. Emily thought she looked kind of pale in spite of her tan.

"Okay, girls," Rachel called out. "Is everybody here? Good! Thoros on the other side of the net."

20

Nancy, Meghan, Janet, Lisa, Ellen, and Beth took their places while the Fillies spread out on Rachel's side. "Remember," Rachel added, "this is the year we're going to show the Long Branch boys that Webster's girls can't be beat!"

Caro glanced at her newly polished nails. "I'm not really into this, you know," she whined.

"I'm not very good, either," Dru whispered to Emily as she took up a position close to the net. "I hope I don't foul up."

"You'll be fine," Emily assured her. "All you have to do is hit the ball over the net when it comes in your direction."

"I'll be playing with the Fillies," Rachel said, "because you Thoros don't need my help. Let's go. Lynda, serve!"

Lynda caught the ball Rachel threw at her and popped it over the net. Beth popped it right back toward Emily. Emily used both hands to return it, delighted that it didn't end up hitting the net. It wasn't a great shot, but in the scramble, the Thoros missed it.

"Score one for the Fillies!" Rachel shouted.

As the game progressed, Emily noticed that Rachel got paler and paler. Suddenly Rachel clutched her stomach and groaned, "Time out, gang. I need a break."

"Are you okay, Rachel?" Emily asked, coming over to where Rachel sat on the ground, her head between her knees.

"Yeah—yeah, I'm fine. . . . No, I'm not." Rachel raised groggy eyes. "I think I'm going to throw up. I feel really *awful*. But I'm sure if I lie down for a while I'll be okay. I better go back to the cabin. . . ."

Emily helped Rachel to her feet and walked with her back up the path toward the cabins. "Maybe I should ask Marie to take a look at you," she said.

"Okay." Rachel grimaced. "Maybe it was something I ate. When I took the Thoros into Winnepac, I had a piece of pizza. Guess that wasn't very smart, considering that we'd just had lunch. Maybe Marie can give me an antacid or something."

But by the time they reached the Thoros' cabin, Rachel's teeth were chattering and she was shivering in spite of the heat. She crawled into her bunk and pulled the blankets up around her. "I'm freezing . . ." she mumbled. But when Emily touched her forehead, it was burning up.

"I'm going to get Marie right away," she said. "Will you be all right while I'm gone?"

Rachel nodded. "S-s-sure. I'll be f-f-fine."

She didn't look fine, Emily thought worriedly. She looked awful! Emily ran as fast as she could for the farmhouse. Once inside, she called Marie's name, but no one answered. She checked out the camp store, the dining room, living room, and finally the kitchen. No Marie. Then Emily heard the whirring and churning of the washing machines in the basement. She dashed down the stairs, to find Marie putting a load of laundry

23

in the dryer. When she saw Emily, she said, "Hi, honey. What's up? Is something the matter?"

"Rachel's sick," Emily said. "Her stomach hurts and she's got chills and fever. She's lying down in the Thoros' cabin. I think you better take a look at her."

"Oh, dear," Marie said, a worried frown creasing her forehead. "Poor thing! I thought she looked a little pale this morning. I only hope it's not the flu—all we need is a flu epidemic just in time for Field Day."

She hurried up the steps ahead of Emily. In her shorts and baggy T-shirt, Emily thought Marie looked like one of the campers even though she had to be about the same age as Emily's mother.

In the kitchen, she said, "I'll go to Rachel right away. You run along, Emily. And thanks for telling me."

"Tell her I hope she feels better," Emily said. "We all do." Then she went out the back door of the farmhouse and took a shortcut across the lawn, hoping she hadn't missed too much of the volleyball game.

Emily needn't have worried. The volleyball game had turned into a squabble between the Thoros and the Fillies about whether or not the last point counted because the ball had bounced off Dru's head and over the net rather than being properly hit. Meghan had turned her ankle, and was sitting on the ground rubbing it and moaning, and Caro was wailing, "I knew it! I just *knew* I'd break a fingernail, and it was my longest one!"

"Can we *please* get on with the game?" Lynda yelled.

24

"Time out—can't you see that Meghan's hurt?" Beth, another Thoro, yelled back. Then she saw Emily and came over to her. "How's Rachel?" she asked.

"She looks pretty sick to me," Emily said. "Marie thinks she may have the flu. She's over at the cabin with her now."

"The flu? Oh, no!" cried Janet. "And she's been *breathing* all over us! We'll *all* get sick!"

"We may not all get sick, but without Rachel, we sure don't stand a chance of beating the boys at volleyball or softball this year," Libby sighed. "Look at us—we're a mess!"

"If Rachel's sick, who's going to teach our riding class?" piped up one of the Foals who had wandered over to watch the game. "How are we going to learn how to play mounted games? We can't practice without Rachel."

"She was going to help me make my witch's hat," Dru added.

"I didn't say Rachel *definitely* had the flu," Emily pointed out. "I said Marie thought she *might*. Maybe, like Rachel said, it was just something she ate." She didn't really think so, but she wanted to cheer everybody up.

"Well, so much for volleyball today anyway," Lynda said, picking up the ball and tucking it under her arm. "Anybody want to swim?"

For the rest of the sports period, the campers practiced swimming and canoeing under Melinda's instruction, but their hearts weren't really in it. When

25

Melinda heard about Rachel, she volunteered to help the Beginners with mounted games that afternoon, so they were taken care of, at least for now.

"But I won't be able to take all their classes if Rachel's really sick," she said. "I help my dad in his hardware store every morning. He really needs me."

"Maybe Marie could take the Beginners in the morning," Danny suggested as the Fillies walked back to their bunkhouse to change into their riding clothes.

"Hey, that's a great idea!" Libby said. "Marie's a really good rider. And maybe Chris or Warren could coach us in softball and volleyball!"

"Warren?" Caro's big, beautiful eyes lit up. "Now *that's* a *really* good idea. Let's see, I could wear my white shorts, and that red-and-white striped rugby shirt . . ."

"I thought sports weren't your thing," Lynda said, raising one eyebrow. "You sure changed your tune pretty fast!"

All the girls knew that Caro had a crush on the Websters' eldest son. They also knew—and Caro did, too—that Melinda was Warren's girl friend. That didn't seem to bother Caro, however. Emily didn't think Warren would be interested in a fourteen-year-old girl, even if he didn't already have a girl friend. Besides, she thought Chris Webster was much nicer than his older brother, though he wasn't quite as handsome. It would really be fun if Chris was their coach, but it didn't seem likely to Emily. The Thoros

26

probably wouldn't pay attention to a boy who was younger than they were, and neither would Caro.

Now Caro tossed her blond ponytail and said, "Why, Lynda, I'm only thinking about Field Day. We don't want to let Webster's down, do we? I may not be a jock like *some* people . . ."—she glanced from Lynda to Libby—" . . . but I'll certainly do my best."

"Oh, brother!" Libby muttered to Emily.

Emily just shrugged. She wasn't terribly interested in Caro at the moment, but she did want to know what was happening with Rachel.

As they passed the Thoros' cabin, Marie came out. She smiled when she saw them, but the smile was a little strained. The girls immediately clustered around her, joined by several Thoros. Everyone spoke at once.

"How's Rachel?"

"Is it the flu?"

"Is she going to be okay?"

Marie raised her hands to ward off further questions. "She's dozing now. She feels pretty awful, and she has a fever of a hundred and one. I'm only an R.N., not a doctor, but it looks like flu to me. I'm going to call her parents—they'll pick her up and take her home." She turned to the Thoros. "That means you'll be on your own tonight, but as you know, Matt and I are always on call if you need us. Meghan tells me that Melinda will take the Foals' practice session this afternoon, and Matt and I will arrange for coverage of the rest of Rachel's duties until she gets well. It may

27

be only a twenty-four-hour bug. On the other hand . . . well, we won't know until Rachel sees her doctor. Try to be *very* quiet in the cabin," she said to the Thoros. "Rest is the best thing for her right now."

Everyone nodded, and the Thoros tiptoed into their bunkhouse as the Fillies headed for theirs and Marie strode off in the direction of the farmhouse.

"Oh, Marie," Caro called after her, "did anything come for me in the mail? Like a package? A *big* package?"

Marie paused and looked over her shoulder. "No, Caro. Why? Is it something important?"

"It's important, all right," Caro said. "But if it didn't come today, it'll probably come tomorrow. Thanks anyway."

What could Caro be waiting for, Emily wondered. Oh, well, it was no big deal. When whatever it was arrived, she was sure Caro would let everyone know.

Chapter Three

Emily stripped out of her wet bathing suit and got into her riding clothes before anyone else. She didn't bother to dry her short, wavy brown hair—it dried quickly in the warm summer air, and she didn't want to hang around, waiting until Caro finished with the blow dryer. Shoving her feet into her boots and grabbing her velvet-covered hard hat, which all the campers were required to wear whenever they rode, she dashed out of the cabin and headed for the stables. Though she'd only ridden Joker that morning, it seemed like ages since she'd seen him, and she always liked to have a few minutes alone with the big, beautiful palomino before the rest of the campers arrived to saddle up their horses and ponies.

As she jogged along the path, Emily felt in the pocket of her jeans to make sure she'd remembered the oatmeal cookie she'd saved for Joker. She always brought him a treat—an apple, a handful of baby carrots from the Websters' vegetable garden, or sometimes, like today, a leftover dessert. Yes, the cookie was there. It was kind of crumbled, but it was definitely there. And Joker wouldn't care if it was crumbled or not.

If only she could make up her mind what her costume would be! She was really sorry that Rachel was sick, and it would be too bad if Webster's didn't make a good showing in volleyball and softball, but the most important thing to Emily right now was to come up with a costume that would be worthy of Joker.

Suddenly Emily skidded to a stop. Pegasus! The legendary winged horse! She could make a pair of huge wings, with multicolored feathers, that would flap gently as Joker moved.

But how could she do that? And what would she wear? From the little Emily knew about Pegasus, he didn't have a rider. And Marie probably didn't have multicolored feathers in her refrigerator box.

Emily resumed her pace. No, that wouldn't be possible. She'd have to think of something else.

By the time she reached the stable, nothing had occurred to her. But that was all right, because Joker stretched his neck out of his stall the minute he heard her footsteps, whickering gently in greeting. Emily was so pleased that she forgot everything else. She took out the crumbled cookie and held it on the flattened palm of her hand so Joker could nibble it. His soft, velvety lips brushed across her hand. As he munched, she scratched between his ears where his silver forelock fell over his big brown eyes, savoring the warmth and scent of him. Emily thought there was nothing in the whole world that smelled as good as a horse. Joker smelled much better than new-mown hay, or roses in bloom, or the expensive perfumes and colognes that Caro used. Emily and Judy had decided that if they could just bottle the essence of horse, every horse lover in the world would buy it by the gallon!

Emily took down Joker's saddle and bridle and let herself into his stall, speaking softly to him. His golden coat was silky smooth—she had groomed him well after her morning riding lesson. Joker stamped and whuffled contentedly as she placed the pad and saddle on his back and fastened the girth, then slipped off his halter and put on his bridle.

"We're going to practice for the mounted games, Joker," she said, stroking his neck. "I guess you know all about them, because you've been doing them for years, but it's all new to me. I'm counting on you to help me because I'm not exactly sure what to do. I know there will be relay races, and musical chairs, and stuff like that, and it sounds like fun. But if I do something stupid, please don't give up on me. I'm doing the best I can, okay?"

Joker nodded his head and snorted as though he understood every word she was saying. Emily threw her arms around his neck and hugged him. How lucky she was to have been given a horse like him!

*   *   *

"Listen up, girls!" Pam Webster called from the center of the Intermediate ring. "For the rest of the week, we're going to concentrate on horsemanship and mounted games. I guess you all know by now that in most of the events, Webster's campers compete against Long Branch according to age. But in horsemanship and mounted games, it's according to experience. So you intermediate riders will be competing with Long Branch boys who are at the same level as you are in riding. Some of them will be older, and some of them will be younger. Our class, the Intermediates, will participate in several relay races during the mounted games."

"Relay races are boring," Meghan said. "All you do is run back and forth, passing a baton to the next person."

"That's not what you do in *these* relay races," Pam said. "You'll be bobbing for apples, and passing the banana."

"Passing the *banana*?" Emily said. "Are you serious, Pam?"

Pam grinned. "Trust me. It's fun. We'll get to that a little later. The first thing we have to practice is the apple bobbing. You'll notice that at the far end of the ring there's a bucket."

Everybody looked. Sure enough, they saw a large blue plastic bucket.

"The bucket is filled with water, and floating in the water are some apples. The first rider on our team—that's going to be you, Meghan—rides as fast as she

32

can to the bucket, gets off her horse, and grabs an apple in her teeth, keeping her hands behind her back. Then she gets back onto her horse, races back to the next person in line—that'll be you, Penny—and hands it over. Penny puts the apple in her mouth, gallops off to the bucket, drops the apple, bites another one, and remounts, going back as fast as she can to the next rider, and so on. Got it?"

"What if we drop the apple?" Danny asked.

"You have to get off your horse and sink your teeth into it. . . ."

Emily got a fit of the giggles. "Into the *horse?*" she asked, and the rest of the riders broke up, too.

Pam gave her a look that was meant to be severe, but she couldn't help grinning. "No, Miss Jordan, *not* into the horse! Into the *apple!*"

When the laughter had subsided into a few muffled snorts, Pam went on. "You sink your teeth into the apple without using your hands, get back on, and deliver it to the next girl. You *can* use your hands for that. Okay, let's begin. Remember, your horses have been doing this for years, so you don't have to worry too much about handling them. They'll stop on a dime, stand still while you dismount and bob for the apple, and be ready to take off the minute you're back in the saddle."

At a signal from Pam, Meghan took off on her sturdy little sorrel at top speed. When she reached the bucket, she leaped off and knelt, trying to bite the floating apple. She finally got it, remounted, and

33

dashed back to Penny. She thrust it into Penny's hand—and Penny dropped it.

"No hands, Penny," Pam called out as Penny scrambled out of Dr. Pepper's saddle and reached for the apple. "*Bite* it!"

Penny bent down and managed to get the apple in her teeth. She got back on Pepper and galloped to the bucket. When she reached it, she pulled Pepper to a halt and sat there, staring wide-eyed at Pam, the apple still in her mouth.

"Wubbleuhdunu?" she mumbled—or at least, that's what it sounded like to Emily.

"What?" Pam asked.

Penny opened her mouth and the apple dropped into her hand. "I said, what do I do now? I forgot what you said."

Pam laughed. "You drop the apple, or toss it over the fence or something, and then you dismount, bite another one, and carry it back to the next rider."

Penny nodded. "Okay. Here goes!"

She threw the tooth-marked apple over the fence, then got off her horse and tried to bite one of the apples that were floating in the bucket. She finally got one and remounted, sputtering and laughing, then dashed back to Danny, who took it and raced off on Misty, her black mare.

"Way to go, Danny!" Emily cried, bouncing excitedly up and down in the saddle. Joker fidgeted a little. He wasn't used to so much activity on his back when

he was standing still. Emily leaned over and patted his satiny shoulder.

"Sorry, Joker," she said softly. "I didn't mean to upset you. But Pam's right—this is fun!"

When it was Emily's turn, Joker took off like a rocket. The minute he stopped by the bucket, Emily leaped out of the saddle and fell on all fours, plunging her face into the water. There were only three apples left, and they all seemed to have a will of their own, evading her snapping teeth. At last she bit into the fattest, reddest one and triumphantly swung herself onto Joker's back, tossing her wet brown hair out of her eyes. Once again, Joker sprang into action, and Emily delivered her apple to Carla, the next girl in line.

"That was great!" Pam shouted when the last rider had completed the course. "I'm really proud of you guys."

"Can we do the banana now?" Meghan asked. She'd apparently forgotten that relay races were supposed to be boring.

"I wish we could, but we can't today," Pam said. "Everything's kind of mixed up since Rachel's sick. Melinda usually helps Mom prepare supper, but she's teaching the Beginners this afternoon, so I'm elected. I have to go up to the house right away."

"Gee, Pam, I didn't know you could cook," Emily said.

Pam made a face. "I can't, but I can help get things ready. And remember—Emily, Penny, and Danny— it's the Fillies' turn for kitchen detail, so please remind the others, okay? You don't have to show up till five, though, so maybe you and the rest of the class would like to check out the Beginners' and Advanced rings. The Beginners are practicing musical chairs, and the Advanced riders are bending."

"Bending?" repeated Karen, one of the Foals. "Bending what?" Emily was wondering the same thing.

"In the bending race, the riders weave in and out between a line of poles that are stuck in the ground," Pam explained. "It's kind of like what skiers do in a slalom, only on horseback and without snow." She headed for the gate that led out of the ring, calling over her shoulder, "Don't forget to cool down your horses and let them out into the pasture. See you later!"

"I want to see the bending," Lisa said.

"Me, too." Meghan followed her out of the ring.

"What do you want to do, Emily?" Danny asked. "Want to watch Libby, Lynda, and Caro bend?"

"Sure, why not?" Emily turned to Penny. "Coming, Penny?"

"No, I think I'll watch musical chairs. I want to see how Dru is doing," Penny said. The rest of the Intermediates, Carla, Karen, and Debby, decided to go with Penny, so Emily and Danny hurried to catch up with Meghan and Lisa.

They lined their mounts up along the fence surrounding the Advanced ring, where Lynda on The Dandy, her dapple gray gelding, was just starting the

37

course. Emily could tell right away why the competition was called a bending race—as Lynda and Dan cantered around pole after pole, both horse and rider *did* bend. When they had rounded the last pole, they retraced their route, and Libby and Foxy took off.

Emily caught her breath. Libby was crouched over Foxy's neck, her bottom sticking up in the air, and Foxy shot forward like a racehorse released from the starting gate. He seemed to be going much too fast, but Libby guided him expertly around the first pole.

"Slow down, Libby!" Matt yelled from the center of the ring. "Speed counts, but you lose points if you knock down a pole. And you'll hurt both yourself and your horse if you fall!"

Libby nodded and slackened Foxy's speed, her small, freckled face intent beneath her velvet hard hat. Though they brushed against one of the poles, they didn't knock any of them down.

"Boy, Libby's really some rider, isn't she?" Danny said admiringly when they had completed the course. "It's like she was *born* in the saddle!"

Caro was the next rider. Her style was completely different from either Libby's or Lynda's. In her beautifully tailored, perfectly fitting breeches and shirt, she was the picture of elegance as she expertly piloted Dark Victory, her dark bay, in and out among the poles. Emily couldn't help being impressed. Caro was very good, no doubt about it.

"I wonder if I'll ever be able to ride like that," Emily sighed.

Then excited squeals and shrieks from the Beginners' ring distracted her attention. It sounded as if musical chairs was a lot of fun.

"Want to see what's happening over there?" she asked Danny.

"Okay. Bending's terrific, but watching all these super riders makes me feel *inferior*, know what I mean?" Danny sighed.

Emily did, but she was determined that some day—maybe next year—she'd be an Advanced rider herself, and she and Joker would be every bit as good as Libby and Foxy, Lynda and Dan, or Caro and Vic.

Emily and Danny rode over to the Beginners' ring where they saw four bales of hay in the center and several more stacked along the fence. The riders who had not yet been eliminated, five in all, were circling the four bales at a sedate walk.

"I don't hear any music," Danny said.

"They don't practice with music," Penny told Danny and Emily. "Melinda claps her hands when it's time to get off and sit down. Look, Dru's still in the running!"

Sure enough, Dru and Donna were among those left in the game. Donna, as usual, looked calm and placid. Dru's round face was flushed and anxious, but she didn't look scared at all. Emily knew that only a few days ago, Dru would most likely have refused to compete at all because she would have been sure she'd make a fool of herself. The other four riders were Foals, and three of them were riding fat little ponies.

39

Emily looked at Melinda, who was standing near the bales of hay. Melinda looked a little anxious too, Emily thought. That was understandable, because Melinda, the Foals' counselor and the camp's water sports instructor, had seldom if ever taught a riding class. Emily guessed that Melinda was probably more comfortable onstage, singing with Warren's rock band, The River Rats, than she was right now.

Suddenly Melinda clapped her hands, and all five riders scrambled off their horses and ponies, dashing for the four bales of hay. The riders who were on the sidelines cheered and shouted encouragement as the players plopped themselves down on the bales. A Foal who was a little slower than the others found herself without a seat, and immediately burst into tears. Melinda ran over to her and hugged the little girl, who wiped her nose with the back of her hand, grabbed her pony's reins, and went sadly to join the other riders who had been eliminated. Dru looked up, saw Penny and Emily, and waved, grinning.

Penny and Emily waved back. "Wouldn't it be neat if Dru won?" Penny said. "I know it's only a practice, but it would be neat anyway."

Emily thought about that. "Yes, it would be nice," she said at last, "but the really important thing is that she's not scared of horses anymore, and that she's happy."

"Yeah, she is, isn't she? And that makes me happy, too," Penny said.

Melinda clapped her hands again, and the four contestants got back on their mounts while she dragged one of the hay bales off to the side.

Emily glanced at her watch. "Hey, it's four-thirty," she said. "We better take our horses back to the stable so we can help Pam and Marie in the kitchen. I'm sure Dru and the rest of the Fillies will remember they're supposed to help out."

As she rode Joker away from the training ring, she said softly to him, "I still haven't figured out what we're going to be for the Costume Parade, but I'm sure I will very soon. If you weren't such a special horse, it'd be easier, but you are, so it's not. I'll think of something worthy of you, honest I will."

But what was it going to be? Emily hadn't the faintest idea.

Chapter Four

After they had cooled down their horses and let them out into the pasture for the night, Emily, Penny, and Danny hurried back to the Fillies' bunkhouse for a quick wash, changed into shorts and T-shirts, and arrived on the dot of five to help Marie and Pam get supper ready. The rest of the Fillies soon joined them. Everybody wanted to know how Rachel was.

"Her parents took her home," Marie told them as she spooned homemade potato salad into two big bowls. "The Orbisons live in Winnepac, so it wasn't much of a trip. They're taking her to the doctor, and they'll call when they find out what's wrong." She sighed. "Rachel was feeling pretty awful, I'm afraid. I'm sure it's either a virus or the flu, so I doubt if she'll be in any condition to return to camp for the rest of the week. Even if it's only a twenty-four-hour bug, she'll be weak and have to rest for a few days."

"We'll manage, Mom," Pam said, handing a platter heaped with chicken salad to Lynda. Since it had been such a hot day, the evening's menu consisted of a variety of salads. At Pam's direction, the Fillies put two tables together in the dining room to serve as an impromptu salad bar.

Caro, who was garnishing the salads with watercress and cherry tomatoes, said, "I guess that means no softball practice after supper, right? That is, unless Warren might be willing to take over."

"As a matter of fact, he's going to do just that," Marie said. She finished tossing yet another salad, this one composed of greens the Foals had picked earlier in the day, and gave the big wooden bowl to Emily.

"Terrific!" Caro said, tossing the rest of the cherry tomatoes on top of the greens. "I can hardly wait!"

"I thought you weren't too crazy about competing with the Long Branch boys," Lynda reminded her. "I seem to remember you saying that sports weren't your thing."

Caro smirked. "I *also* said that I didn't intend to let Webster's down. And I'm sure, with Warren coaching us, that we'll do just fine. We'll make so many touchdowns that those Long Branch boys will be *green* with envy."

Libby rolled her eyes. "Caro, you don't make touchdowns in softball. That's *football.* In softball, you make *runs*."

"Whatever." Caro examined the salads critically, her head cocked to one side, then placed one sprig of watercress in the middle of the chicken salad. "There! It looks lovely. You can take it out now, Lynda."

"Thanks a bunch," Lynda mumbled. "Aren't we lucky to have somebody with such an artistic sense!"

Caro smiled. "Yes, you are."

Little more than an hour later, the Fillies and Thoros had assembled on the softball field. The Foals were working on their costumes with the help of Melinda and Marie.

Warren Webster, in jeans and a sleeveless T-shirt, was waiting impatiently for them, hands on hips. He didn't look particularly pleased with his new assignment.

"Okay, girls," he sighed. "You're gonna be playing against Long Branch's Seniors and Intermediates, and I have to tell you that it's not gonna be easy. Those guys are bigger and stronger, and they're probably better at the game than you are. How many of you have ever played softball before?"

Ten hands shot up, Emily's among them. Caro's wasn't one of them. Neither was Dru's.

"I'm the captain of the girls' softball team at my school," Lynda said.

Warren nodded. "Can you pitch?"

"Oh, yeah!" Lynda assured him. "Back home, I always pitch!"

"I play first base," Janet added.

"I'm a shortstop," Beth put in.

44

"I can play *any* position," Libby called out.

Emily said, "I'm usually at third base."

"Okay, we have seven Fillies and six Thoros, and for practice I guess you'll have to play against each other even though we don't have enough men—uh, I mean girls—for two teams. Lynda, you pitch for the Fillies."

"I can pitch for the Thoros," Nancy said. Emily didn't know her very well, but she was a stocky, well-muscled girl who looked like a jock.

"We better get started," Warren said, looking at his watch. "The River Rats are practicing tonight, so I have to cut out of here by eight. That gives us about an hour."

"Oh, Warren, when's your band's next gig?" Caro asked, fluttering her lashes. She was wearing her white shorts and rugby shirt, as planned. When Caro heard Warren was coaching the team she had run back to the cabin after dinner to change. Her silky blond hair was fastened in a ponytail on the top of her head, and pale golden wisps framed her exquisite face. Emily thought she looked gorgeous, and at least sixteen, but Warren didn't seem to notice.

"Next week," he said. "Okay, Fillies at bat first, Thoros in the field."

"Super!" Caro cried. "I can't wait!"

" 'Fraid you'll have to. We're playing in Eltonburg—that's fifty miles away." He assigned positions, and the Thoros trotted off while the Fillies clustered around Warren.

"What's the batting order?" Libby asked, adjusting the visor of her blue baseball cap.

"Good question." Warren looked at the seven Fillies, then shrugged. "You start off, Libby, then Penny, Emily, Caro, Lynda, Danny, and Dru."

"I've never played softball before," Dru whispered, looking anxious.

"I haven't, either," Caro said to Warren. "But I'm sure you can teach me what to do."

"*I've* played," Penny said proudly. "Twice! Or maybe three times."

Warren groaned softly. "Maybe I ought to run over the rules of the game. The pitcher throws the ball over the plate. The batter tries to hit it. If she misses, it's a strike. If she hits it . . ."—he looked as if he thought that was extremely unlikely—" . . . and it's fair, and nobody on the other team catches it before it hits the ground, she runs to first base—or second, or third, if it's a really long drive . . ."

"Uh, Warren, which one is first base?" Dru asked.

"The one to your right," Warren sighed, "where Janet's standing."

When he had finished his explanation, he said, "Batter up!" and Libby stepped to the plate, swinging her bat ferociously. She connected with Nancy's first pitch, sending the ball into right field. Ellen missed it, and Libby scored a double. Penny hit a single, much to her astonishment, which moved Libby to third base. Then Emily flied out.

"Rats!" she muttered.

Caro was next in the batting order. She picked up the bat and rested it on her shoulder, gazing up at Warren. "Am I holding it right?" she asked. Warren moved behind her, showing her how to place her hands on the bat. "You mean like this?" Caro swung, narrowly missing Warren's head.

"You're supposed to hit the *ball*, not the coach!" Warren yelled.

"I was just practicing," Caro said, pouting prettily. "Maybe you'd better show me again."

"No way! Just do your best," Warren said, hastily stepping out of range.

Caro struck out. Then Lynda hit a liner to the outfield, and Libby scored while the Fillies cheered and applauded.

"That wasn't fair," Beth complained. "It bounced off a molehill. Can't we do it again?"

"*No!*" Warren hollered. "Molehills don't count. A run is a run. Play ball!"

Danny struck out, and the Fillies took the field. Janet, the first Thoro at bat, hit a ball straight at Caro, who squealed and danced aside, wailing, "My *nails!*"

Janet's hit was a home run, Meghan flied out, and the next two Thoros struck out to retire the side. In the course of the next two innings, neither team scored a single run. Then Lynda hit a foul ball into a patch of poison ivy. None of the Thoros would go near it, so Warren called the game.

"Fillies one, Thoros one," he sighed, shaking his head in despair. "It beats me how you girls can ride so well, and be so uncoordinated at a simple game like softball."

"It's *not* simple!" Caro grumbled. Her white shorts and shirt were dusty and covered with grass stains from the many times she'd fallen, running after—or from—a ball, and her ponytail was coming down. "There are so many things to remember, like how many strikes you get before you're out, and why it doesn't count if you hit the stupid ball one place instead of another. And the bat is so heavy and *clumsy*, and the ball weighs a *ton.* . . ."

"I think I pulled something in my shoulder," Danny added, wincing.

"I'm going to ask Marie for an Ace bandage," Meghan said. "I twisted my ankle again. If we're playing tomorrow, count me out!"

"I was eaten alive by mosquitoes when I was playing third base," Ellen complained as she scratched several welts on her arms. "At least when you're riding you can *outrun* the mosquitoes!"

"What it really comes down to, I think," Emily told Warren shyly, "is that we all *love* our horses so much that we work extra hard at riding well."

"Yes—it's kinda hard to love a softball," Penny put in.

Libby grinned. *"Hate* it, then! Look at it this way— softballs are covered with horsehide, so every time you get a hit, you're getting revenge for some poor dead horse."

Warren grabbed several bats and mitts. "Listen, I

really have to go or I'm going to be late for practice." He looked around at the campers in the fading light. "Sorry if I was a little rough on you. You weren't all that bad."

He strode off, and the Fillies and Thoros gathered up the rest of the equipment and straggled after him. Emily fell in step with Libby.

"Is that true, what you said about softballs being covered with horsehide?" she asked, wide-eyed.

"Yep," Libby replied. "Or at least they used to be. Baseballs, too. Maybe they use something else now, like Naugahyde."

Emily shuddered. "That's gross! We shouldn't be playing softball *at all*, not at Webster's!"

"That's ridiculous," Nancy said irritably. "A ball's a ball. And softball is really fun when you get the hang of it."

"I don't see why they call it softball," Caro said. "There's nothing soft about it!"

"What are volleyballs made of?" Penny asked, looking apprehensive.

Nancy said quickly, "I don't know, and it doesn't matter. What *does* matter is that if we don't shape up, we're going to look like idiots out there on Sunday." Lisa, Beth and the other Thoros groaned in agreement.

"We aren't very good, are we?" Dru sighed. "And I don't think Warren's going to keep on coaching us. He didn't seem to be enjoying it very much."

"Well, neither was I!" Caro snapped. "I think he was *extremely* rude."

"I wish my friend Judy was here," Emily said. "She's an all-around athlete, not like me."

"You did all right, Emily," Lynda said. "Maybe next time you'll get a run."

"I wouldn't count on it." Nancy scowled at Emily, Caro, Penny, Dru, and Danny. "You guys play like—like *Foals!*"

"Well, at least we don't *look* like horses, like *some* people I could mention!" Caro shot back.

"Nancy, that wasn't very nice, what you just said," Libby added.

"Well, it's true," Lisa said. "Face it, the only Fillies who are any good at all are you and Lynda. The rest of them are just impossible. With all that dead wood on our team, we might as well give up before we start!"

"That's fine by me!" Caro snapped. "I don't have to stand here and be insulted. I hate team sports, anyway! Coming, Danny?"

Danny nodded and the two of them marched off toward the farmhouse, noses in the air.

Dru's lower lip was trembling. She looked close to tears. "I *said* I'd never played before," she mumbled. With Penny at her side, she followed Caro and Danny.

Libby pulled down the visor of her baseball cap and glared at Lisa and Nancy. "Like my grandmother says, it's not whether you win or lose, it's how you play the game. Remember, Lisa, when we play the Long

51

Branch boys, we're all going to be on the same side whether you like it or not, so we better start developing some team spirit."

" 'Team spirit!' That's a laugh," Janet said. "We don't even have a coach! And most of the Fillies probably wouldn't be able to hit the ball if we did."

"Oh, yeah?" Lynda came over to stand by Libby. "The Thoros aren't so terrific, either. All Ellen did was scratch her mosquito bites, and Meghan was limping all over the place!"

"Now just a minute!" Meghan said angrily. "It's not my fault I twisted my ankle."

"And I didn't ask every mosquito in the Adirondacks to zero in on me, either," Ellen whined. "What's the matter with you, Lynda? Lisa said you and Libby play pretty well. Why are you so mad?"

"Because Fillies stand up for each other!" Lynda said, her brown eyes blazing. "We're friends! It's like the Three Musketeers—'All for one and one for all.' "

"Oh, gimme a break!" Nancy sighed. "Lisa's right— the rest of the Fillies stink. And come to think of it, your pitching wasn't so hot, either."

"Then how come you couldn't hit anything?" Libby asked with a ferocious grin.

All this bickering was getting to Emily. Before Nancy could reply, she said quickly, "Hey, guys, let's hurry up. We're going to be late for campfire!"

Nobody said anything more as the girls trooped up to the farmhouse, Thoros in one group and the three remaining Fillies in another. They dropped their bats and mitts in the front hall and headed for the campfire site. As they approached the picnic grove, they could hear the Foals singing, accompanied by a guitar. Emily assumed it was Chris's, since Warren had already left.

There were three jolly fishermen,
There were three jolly fishermen,
Fisher, fisher men, men, men!
Fisher, fisher men, men, men!
There were three jolly fishermen . . .

Emily didn't feel very jolly. For the first time since she'd come to Webster's, the Fillies and the Thoros were being nasty to each other, and she didn't like it one bit. The Thoros made a point of sitting together in a group on the far side of the campfire, so the Fillies sat next to the Foals and began to sing:

The first one's name was I-Isaac,
The first one's name was I-Isaac,
I-I-saac, saac, saac!
I-I-saac, saac, saac!
The first one's name was I-Isaac.

"There was nothing wrong with my pitching," Lynda grumbled. "Nancy thinks she's such a great athlete—you oughta see her ride! She almost fell off today when we were practicing bending!"

"You're a terrific pitcher," Emily said. "C'mon, Lynda—sing."

The second one's name was Abraham,
The second one's name was Abraham,

53

Abra, Abra ham, ham, ham!
Abra, Abra ham, ham, ham!
The second one's name was Abraham.

"Dead wood, huh?" Caro muttered to Danny. "I just can't *believe* those Thoros! You'd think Ellen and Beth would have had something nice to say—after all, they're supposed to be my *friends!*"

The third one's name was Ja-a-cob,
The third one's name was Ja-a-cob,
Ja-a-cob, cob, cob!
Ja-a-cob, cob, cob!
The third one's name was Ja-a-cob.

"We'll show 'em we're as good as they are," Libby said to Emily. "All we need is a little practice."

"But who's going to coach us?" Emily asked.

Libby shrugged. "Matt and Marie will find somebody sooner or later."

"I hope it's sooner, because later may be *too* late," Emily sighed.

They all went down to Amster . . . ssh!
They all went down to Amster . . . ssh!
Amster, Amster . . . ssh! Ssh! Sssh!

Dru leaned over to Penny and said softly, "I don't want to play in the softball game. I'll only do something stupid."

"Me, too," Penny whispered back.

You must not say that naughty word!
You must not say that naughty word!

54

Naughty, naughty word, word, word!
Naughty, naughty word, word, word!

"I came to Webster's to ride horses, not to hit some dumb ball around," Danny said.

I'm going to say it anyhow.
I'm going to say it anyhow.
Any, any how, how, how!
Any, any how, how, how!

"I think we ought to learn to play polo," Caro murmured. "Now *there's* a sport I could really relate to!"

They all went down to Amsterdam!
They all went down to Amsterdam!
Amster, Amster dam, dam, dam!
Amster, Amster dam, dam, dam!
They all went down to Amsterdam!

Emily tilted her head back and looked up into the night sky. High above, she saw the evening star. She closed her eyes tight and said to herself, "Star light, star bright, first star I see tonight, wish I may, wish I might, have the wish I wish tonight. I wish . . . I wish everybody would stop being mad at each other. I wish Rachel would get better fast. And I wish, oh how I wish that I could decide what I'm going to be for the Costume Parade!"

"You okay, Emily?" Libby asked.

Emily opened her eyes and nodded. "I'm fine. Just wishing, that's all."

Chapter Five

It was obvious from the moment the Thoros and Fillies entered the dining room the next morning for breakfast that they were definitely on opposite sides in the Battle of the Ballgame. Ellen and Beth, who had been Caro's special friends among the Thoros, didn't ask her to sit with them as they usually did. The Thoros sat at one table and the Fillies at another after they had helped themselves to the tempting selection of pancakes, scrambled eggs, bacon, cold cereal, and fresh fruit Marie and the Foals had set out buffet style.

Emily stared at her bowl of granola, milk, and fat red strawberries, but she didn't feel very hungry. Even Dru, who always ate more than the other Fillies, was just playing with the pile of scrambled eggs on her plate while her bacon got cold.

Pam looked around at the seven glum faces and sighed. "Come on, girls. Just because you and the

Thoros had an argument last night is no reason to sit there and mope. Okay, so maybe the Fillies aren't the greatest ballplayers in the world . . ."

"Libby and Lynda are," Penny said. "They're just as good as the Thoros—maybe better!"

"And Meghan and Ellen are just as bad as the rest of us—maybe worse," Danny added.

"That's not the point," Pam said. "The point is that on Field Day you're all going to be on the same team, so everybody has to work together."

"Tell that to the Thoros," Lynda said, scowling.

"Yeah, and good luck," Libby said. "I told them the same thing last night, and it went over like a lead balloon."

"I think we ought to cancel everything except the horsemanship classes and the mounted games," Caro added, daintily taking a bite of her pancake. "Webster's always loses at everything else anyway, and I for one *hate* to lose."

"Nobody much *likes* to lose, Caro," Pam pointed out. "But it's important for us all to do our best, win or lose."

"You're right," Lynda said. "But how *can* we do our best if we don't have a coach?"

"Why don't you coach us, Pam?" Libby asked. "You're real athletic. I bet you could do it."

Pam shook her head. "Thanks for the vote of confidence, but I'm too busy. I have lots of chores to do, and so do Mom and Dad and my brothers. Don't forget that Webster's isn't only a horse camp. It's also a working farm, and that means we *work*, all of us, to keep things going."

"I guess Rachel's pretty important, isn't she?" Penny said. "I mean, she teaches the Foals' riding class, and she coaches us in softball and volleyball, and she helps with the costumes for the Costume Parade."

Dru nibbled at a piece of bacon, looking sad. "I guess I won't be able to be the Wicked Witch without Rachel. And I'll *never* be able to make a Flying Monkey costume for Donna."

"Mom will help you when she has time, and so will Melinda and I," Pam said. "We'll help everybody whenever we can. Speaking of costumes," she added, "have you all decided what you're going to be for the Costume Parade? There are all kinds of awards, you know—for the funniest, the prettiest, the most original, and so forth."

This topic changed the glum atmosphere around the table as all the Fillies excitedly told Pam about their costumes—all except Emily and Caro.

"What about you, Emily?" Pam asked.

"I don't know yet," Emily sighed. "I just can't seem to come up with anything that's good enough—good enough for Joker, that is. He deserves something really fantastic."

"*My* costume is going to be totally stupendous," Caro said with a mysterious smile. "But I'm not going to tell anybody about it. You'll just have to wait and see."

Just then, Matt stood up from where he had been

sitting at the Thoros' table and tapped his knife on a glass to get the campers' attention. When their chatter had died down, he said, "You all know by now that Rachel's sick, and probably won't be coming back to Webster's until next week. That means we're going to be a little shorthanded for the next few days, so Marie and I are counting on you to bear with us if things aren't quite as well organized as usual."

"Who's going to teach the Beginners' riding class?" one of the Foals called out.

"Marie will take your morning class," Matt replied, "and Melinda will help you practice for the mounted games."

That made the Foals happy, but Dru tentatively raised her hand.

"Yes, Dru?"

"Uh . . . if Marie's going to be teaching, who's going to fix lunch?" Dru asked anxiously.

"Honestly, Dru!" Caro sighed. "Can't you think about anything except food? You're supposed to be on a diet, remember?"

Dru stuck out her lower lip. "Yes, but I don't want to *starve* to death!"

Matt grinned. "Nobody's going to starve, believe me. We've arranged to have a friend of ours prepare the noon meals for the rest of the week. Her name is Barbara Casey, and she's the dietician at Winnepac High."

There was a loud chorus of groans from the Thoros.

"Cafeteria food? Yuck!" Ellen said.

59

"Barbara is an excellent cook," Matt said sternly, frowning at the Thoros. "And since your group is on kitchen detail for lunch today, I expect you all to help her out as much as possible—*cheerfully.*"

The Thoros nodded. They all looked a little embarrassed, Emily thought.

"Marie, Pam, and Melinda will divide up the rest of Rachel's duties," Matt went on, addressing all the campers, "and Warren, Chris, and I will do what we can to help out. Afraid we won't be much good at sewing costumes, though!"

Everybody laughed.

"That's about it for now, I guess. . . . Oh, one other thing. I know the Fillies and Thoros are concerned about who's going to coach them in volleyball and softball. All I can say is, we're working on it, but there won't be practice today. Everybody can concentrate on water sports this afternoon, and work on their costumes after lunch. Now if you're all finished eating, the Fillies can help clean up. Riding class as usual in forty-five minutes."

The Foals and Thoros dashed off while the Fillies began to clear the tables and carry the dirty dishes into the kitchen, where they helped Marie stack them in the two big dishwashers.

"Oh, Marie," Caro said, "I'm expecting a package in the mail today, a *big* one. Will you let me know when it comes?"

Marie nodded. "Sure, Caro. You told me about this package yesterday. It's not food, is it? Because if it is, it'll have to go into the refrigerator till you can pick it up."

"No, it's not food," Caro replied. "It's something I asked our housekeeper to send me from home. She's keeping an eye on things while everybody's away—my parents are in Europe, you know."

"Yes, Caro, we know," the rest of the Fillies said in unison.

"Well, I wasn't sure *Marie* did," Caro said huffily. "There, I've done my bit. See you at the stables."

"Hey, Caro, we haven't cleared all the tables yet," Libby called after her, but Caro didn't seem to hear her.

When Emily rode Joker into the intermediate training ring later that morning, she was feeling a little apprehensive. She hoped Meghan and Lisa wouldn't still be in bad moods. In the bright morning sunshine, last night's argument seemed just plain silly. As the girls walked their horses around the ring, Emily came up next to Meghan, deciding to be so friendly that the older girl wouldn't be able to ignore her.

"Hi, Meghan. How's your ankle?" she asked with a smile.

"My ankle?" Meghan looked puzzled.

"Yes—the one you twisted yesterday. Is it feeling better?"

"Oh, yes, much better," Meghan said. "I didn't need an Ace bandage after all." She glanced across the ring at Lisa, then confided to Emily, "To tell the truth, it didn't hurt as much as I pretended it did."

"Then why did you pretend?" Emily asked.

"Well . . . most of the Thoros are really into sports, and I'm not. I have two left feet and butterfingers! I'm okay on a horse, and I'm a pretty decent swimmer, but put me on a ballfield and I'm hopeless. I didn't want Nancy and Janet to get mad at me, so . . ." She shrugged.

Emily grinned. "I understand. I'm exactly the same way."

"Emily, Meghan, single file, please," Pam called from the center of the ring, and Emily held Joker back, falling into line behind Meghan and her horse, Diamond. She was glad there was at least one Thoro who was still speaking to the Fillies.

"Okay, girls," Pam said now. "Bring your horses over here while I fill you in on what we're going to be doing today."

Everybody did.

"We're going to act like this is the real thing, the way it'll be on Sunday in the horsemanship class. Pretend I'm Dad . . ."

Two of the Foals giggled, but Emily thought that wouldn't be too hard—Pam looked more like her father than her mother.

" . . . and do everything I say. Remember, everything counts—your seat, your hands, the position of your feet, the way you handle your mount. There won't be anything tricky, difficult, or different from

62

what you've been doing every day for the past two weeks, so there's nothing to be worried about. Your horses know exactly what to do, but if you don't give them the proper signals, they'll get confused. If you're doing something wrong, I'll let you know, but we won't stop unless somebody has a major problem.

"Okay, let's get started. Lisa, you lead off and the rest will follow."

From then on, Emily concentrated on nothing but putting Joker through his paces and handling him as expertly as she knew how. It would be so wonderful if they won a blue ribbon on Field Day! If they didn't, it certainly wouldn't be Joker's fault. They walked, trotted, and cantered on command, and Emily even got Joker on the proper lead when they went directly into a canter from a walk, something she'd been trying to do for a week. Then she guided Joker through a series of figure eights, being very careful not to twist her body, swing her arms, or pull hard on the reins. Danny and Penny seemed to being doing fine, too, though when Penny and Pepper made a figure eight at a slow canter, Penny leaned so far to the side on the turns that Emily was afraid she'd slide right off.

"Easy, Penny," Pam called. "Remember your center of gravity! Keep your body exactly in line with the angle of your horse when you take him around a turn . . . Meghan, watch those elbows! Don't clamp them to your sides like you're afraid they might fall off . . . Debbie, shorten up on your reins—that's the way . . . *Right* lead, Karen! Slow Pinball to a walk, then

start again . . . Great! You got it! . . . Good, Emily, but try to relax your spine. Who're you going to be for the Costume Parade—the Hunchback of Notre Dame?"

Everybody laughed, but Pam's joke only reminded Emily that she still hadn't decided on her costume.

"I'm thinking, Joker, honest I am," she whispered to her horse, patting his shoulder. His golden coat was dark with sweat—today wasn't any cooler than yesterday had been. Taking the reins in one hand, Emily wiped her face with the other. Perspiration was pouring down from under her riding hat, and her pale blue polo shirt was sticking to her back. But she didn't mind the heat on her own account. It was Joker she was concerned about. After all, the only thing she had to do was sit there, while he had to run around in the hot sun with a hundred pounds of Emily on his back, not to mention the weight of his saddle. Could horses get sunstroke? she wondered. She'd feel just *awful* if anything happened to Joker.

But Pam didn't seem to be worried, so Emily guessed that meant it was all right. And when Pam asked several of the riders to help her set up the jumps, Emily was sure of it. She still felt sorry for Joker, though, and promised him a cool sponge bath when class was over.

Emily, Danny, Penny, and the rest of the Intermediates were riding back to the stable an hour later, feeling pleased with themselves since Pam had been happy with their performance. Then Emily saw the

65

Advanced riders coming out of their ring, so she slowed Joker to a stop, waiting for Libby, Lynda, and Caro.

"How'd it go?" she asked as Libby rode up next to her on Foxy. "Did you just about melt? We did!"

Libby's usually cheerful face looked grim. "I can't *believe* those Thoros!" she muttered, yanking off her riding hat and slinging it over her arm by the chin strap. "You should have heard Nancy and Janet! Just because Dan knocked down the top rail of a double-bar jump the second time around, they started making cracks!"

"Like what?" Danny asked, joining them on Misty, her black mare.

"Oh, like, 'The big-shot athlete isn't so terrific on a horse, either,' and stuff like that."

"What did Matt say?" Emily asked.

"He didn't hear them," Libby said. "I don't know what's wrong with them! They're the nastiest bunch of Thoros I've ever met, and I've been coming to Webster's for *years!*"

Emily sighed. "Maybe it's just the heat. People get irritable when it's so hot." But she really couldn't understand why all the Thoros were making such a big deal about everything. If the Fillies weren't the greatest softball players in the world, and volleyball wasn't their thing either, so what? Would it be the end of the world if the Long Branch boys won those games?

"Oh, Emily, stop being such a Pollyanna," Caro snapped as she came up on Emily's other side. "Those girls are just plain *mean*! I think they're jealous because *some* of the Fillies—" she delicately wiped beads of perspiration from her upper lip"—are more attractive than they are, and they're afraid the Long Branch boys won't be interested in them. And they're right! I mean, what boy in his right mind would have anything to do with a girl who can beat him in softball?"

"Caro, have you always been boy-crazy?" Libby asked.

"I am *not* boy-crazy!" Caro said. "I just like to be appreciated, that's all." Then she smiled. "And I will be, you'll see. Wait till those guys see my costume. They'll flip out!"

"What's it going to be?" Penny called out. She and Pepper were right behind Caro, and she had been listening to every word.

But Caro just shook her head. "Ask me no questions, I'll tell you no lies . . ." She glanced at Libby, grinning. "Like your grandmother probably says!"

Chapter Six

"I don't feel so good," Dru complained. "Maybe I'm coming down with Rachel's bug."

It was shortly after lunch, and the Fillies, along with the Thoros and Foals, were in the big Activity Room behind the farmhouse. The various groups were working on their costumes, and Melinda and Pam were trying their best to help. Emily, who had been picking through the contents of the refrigerator box, hoping to be inspired by something she might find there, looked up. "My stomach's kind of wobbly, too," she admitted.

"I think it was the macaroni salad," Lynda said. "It didn't taste all that great."

"Or maybe it was the chili," Danny added, making a face. "It was just like the chili we get in the school cafeteria back home, and it always upsets my stomach."

68

Libby sighed. "Barbara may be one of Matt and Marie's best friends, but she's not the greatest cook in the world, no matter what they say." She was trying to cover her velvet hard hat with bright yellow satin to make it look like a jockey's cap, and wasn't succeeding. "*Ouch!* I stuck my finger with this dopey needle, and now I'm bleeding all over the place."

"Here's a Band-Aid," Dru suggested, passing one to her. "I've used lots of them already." She certainly had—every one of her fingers was bandaged. "I'm just not very good at sewing. Donna's Flying Monkey suit is gonna be just *awful!*"

"Where's Caro?" Emily asked. "Is she working on that secret costume of hers somewhere else?"

Lynda shrugged. "Search me. Who cares? Oh, nuts! Why won't this foil stick to this bottle? It keeps coming off."

"Maybe it's because you're using too much glue. What about trying Scotch tape?" Emily suggested. She was trying to be helpful to all the Fillies because she figured if she looked busy, nobody would pester her with questions about what her costume was going to be. She still didn't know, and there wasn't much left in Marie's box.

"I give up!" Libby exclaimed, tossing down her hat. "I think I'm just going to forget about a jockey cap, and try to sew some of this yellow satin onto that old blue blouse of Marie's. But it'll probably be a disaster."

69

"Here comes Marie now," Danny said. "I bet she'll help you."

"Libby," Marie said, smiling broadly, "I have a terrific surprise for you!"

"You just found a jockey outfit at a rummage sale, and it'll fit me perfectly?" Libby said hopefully.

Marie shook her head. "Nope. Better than that. Guess who just arrived? Guess who's going to stay with us until Field Day is over? Guess who decided she didn't want to go on a fishing trip with your grandfather, and told him to drop her off here?"

Libby's pert, freckled face lit up like a light bulb. *"Gram?"* she cried.

"You got it, honey!" an unfamiliar voice replied.

All the Fillies stared as a small, wiry woman with short, curly gray hair strode over to Libby and gave her a great big hug. She had to be in her late sixties, Emily figured, but she didn't look like any other grandmother Emily had ever seen. This lady was wearing faded jeans, high-top sneakers, and a bright red T-shirt. Emily's grandmother would never have been caught dead in clothes like that! Libby's Gram was either very tanned, or the freckles that covered her face and arms had all run together to produce the same effect. And her bright blue eyes twinkled like twin sapphires. Emily was aware that her mouth was hanging open, and she abruptly closed it, as Libby and her grandmother jumped up and down in each other's arms.

"Gram, this is fabulous!" Libby shouted. "You're

really gonna be here for Field Day? Wonderful! But where are you staying?"

"Well," Marie said before Gram could answer, "I've asked her to stay here—in the empty bunk in your cabin. Then Pam can move into Rachel's bunk with the Thoros. And she's said she will."

"Yep, that's what I said, all right," Gram said, grinning. "Unless you'd rather I didn't, Libby. I can always get a room at that dinky little motel in Winnepac."

"Hey, don't let her do that!" Lynda cried, running over to embrace Gram. "How you doing, Gram? I haven't seen you for a whole *year!*"

The old woman released Libby and turned to Lynda, giving her a hug, too. "Lynda, baby, you've *grown!* You're so tall and beautiful! How's your heifer?"

"Bluebell's great! I won first prize with her in the Four-H show this spring."

"Congratulations." Gram hugged her again, then let her go. Hands on hips, she looked at the rest of the Fillies. "These are going to be my bunkmates, right? So introduce me, Libby."

Libby did, though Emily was sure Gram couldn't possibly remember everyone's names. Old people's memories got weird after a while. But she was wrong.

"Emily," Gram said, shaking her hand vigorously. "Libby's written to her grandfather and me, and she's told us all about you. You're the one who put the bug in Caro's bunk, right?"

Emily blushed. "Uh . . . well, I guess I kind of did."

71

She hadn't told her parents about that, much less her grandparents, though she'd told Judy everything about it.

"I did the same kind of thing when I was your age," Gram said cheerfully. "Scared the daylights out of her, didn't it?"

Emily giggled. "It sure did!"

"So where's Caro? I've been looking forward to meeting her."

"She's not here, but you'll meet her very soon," Libby said.

"Fine by me," Gram said. That penetrating blue gaze fell on Dru's bandaged fingers. "What happened to you?"

Stammering at first, then gaining confidence as Gram listened intently to what she had to say, Dru told her about her problem with Donna's Flying Monkey costume.

"Forget about it," Gram said briskly. "Concentrate on your own costume, and make a long, thin, curly tail for your horse. That ought to do it. You know," she added, looking Dru up and down, "seems to me you'd make a better Dorothy than you would a Wicked Witch. You're too pretty to be a witch."

Dru stared at her, wide-eyed. "Me? Pretty? With these braces?"

"What do braces matter? When they come off, you'll have the best smile in town. Wish I'd had braces when I was young. Then maybe my teeth wouldn't be crooked as a split-rail fence." Gram grinned. "But

72

crooked or not, they're all mine, and a bird in the hand is worth two in the bush."

Emily couldn't quite see the connection, but it didn't really matter. The important thing was that Dru's round face was flushed with pleasure. She really *did* look pretty, even without the makeup Caro sometimes persuaded her to wear.

"Thanks, Mrs. Dexter," Dru said softly.

"Call me Gram. *Everybody* call me Gram. For the next few days, I'm everyone's grandmother, okay?"

The Fillies all nodded eagerly as Gram went on, "Come to think of it, Dru, you might be a wonderful Dorothy, but I guess it'd be harder to turn your horse into her little dog, Toto, than it would to give Donna a Flying Monkey tail."

"Will you help me make a witch's hat?" Dru asked.

"No problem. I'll be glad to give you a hand. I'll help anybody who needs me. Used to make all my own costumes when I was a bareback rider in the circus. My mother taught me to sew, and my father taught me to ride horses. He also taught me to play just about every sport there is. Mother thought he was crazy—in those days girls weren't supposed to do things like that—but he disagreed."

"I'm going to be a bareback rider," Penny said. "I have a really good costume, but it doesn't fit quite right. Maybe you could—"

"Be glad to," Gram said.

"Gram . . ." Lynda's eyes were shining. "Do you know how to play volleyball and softball?"

73

"Do I ever! Maybe Libby didn't mention it, but for a while there, I was athletic coach for a girls' school. Volleyball and softball? Better believe it!"

"Wow!" Lynda beamed. "Gram, you came just in time!"

"I thought maybe I had." Gram looked at the various parts of the Fillies' costumes that were strewn all over the table. "Yep, I can see you all need help. Guess I have to earn my keep, so let's see what I can do."

The girls all clustered around her, explaining what needed to be worked on, but Emily hung back. Since she didn't know what her costume was going to be, she didn't have anything to say.

Gram noticed her silence. Glancing up from the Indian headband she was making for Danny, she said, "What about you, Emily? Who are you going to be?"

"I haven't decided yet," Emily said. Every time anyone asked her and she gave the same reply, she felt dumber and dumber.

"You want to come up with something really special, don't you? Not because you want to win the grand prize, but because you want your costume to show off your *horse,* not you, right?"

Emily blinked in astonishment. "How—how did you know?" she stammered.

Gram laughed heartily. "I guess Libby didn't mention that, either. When I wasn't riding bareback with that circus, I doubled as a mind-reader in one of the side shows. 'Madame Beatrice—Knows All, Tells All.' "

74

"Really?" Emily gasped.

"Really," Gram said. "But in this case, that's not the real reason I know what you're thinking. Libby's written to me about how crazy you are about that palomino of yours, so I just put two and two together." She smiled at Emily. "We'll talk about it, and I bet we'll figure something out. After all, two heads are better than one."

Emily grinned. "Especially when mine's a cabbage head! Thanks, Gram."

Suddenly a fresh, dry breeze began blowing through the open windows of the Activity Room. It was the first break in the heat for days, and Emily felt her spirits lifting. She couldn't help thinking that Libby's wonderful, oddball grandmother just might have brought the cool air with her, tucked away in a corner of her suitcase. If she *had* a suitcase, that is. Somehow Emily pictured Gram's arrival at Webster's like Mary Poppins's landing on the doorstep of the Banks family, complete with a parrot-head umbrella and a carpetbag filled with all sorts of magical treats. If anybody could help Emily decide on the perfect costume, she was sure it would be Gram.

Several hours later, after water sports and practice for the mounted games, the Fillies straggled into their cabin to find Libby's grandmother sitting on the bunk over Caro's, busily working on Dru's witch's hat. The fan on the windowsill was drawing cool, pine-scented air into the room, and there was a bouquet of wild

75

flowers in a mayonnaise jar on one of the bureaus. Gram responded to the girls' greetings with a wave.

"How'd it go?" she asked cheerfully. "Think you'll beat Long Branch in those relay races and stuff?"

"If we don't it'll be the first time in history," Libby said, tossing her riding hat up onto her bunk.

"Pam taught us the banana race," Emily added. "It was even more fun than the apple dunking!"

Gram looked puzzled. "Banana race? I didn't know bananas could run." Emily could tell right away that she was teasing.

"Oh, Gram!" Libby laughed. "You remember the banana race, don't you? I was in it last year, when I was an Intermediate. The riders pass a banana back and forth instead of a stick or something, and the team that finishes first with the least squashed banana wins."

Gram cocked her head to one side. "Yes, I remember now. I felt mighty sorry for that poor banana!"

"Who's *that?*" Caro, the last of the Fillies to arrive, stood in the doorway clutching a big package to her chest and staring at Gram.

The little gray-haired woman sprang from the upper bunk to the floor, smiling. "Hi, Caro. My, you're even more attractive than Libby said. Love your hair. Is it natural?"

Caro looked confused and a little hostile. "Yes, it's natural. Who *are* you, anyway?"

"I'm Libby's grandmother. I'll be staying here until Field Day is over, and the only available bunk was the

76

one over yours. Hope you don't mind. You can call me Gram—everyone does."

"Uh . . . how do you do?" Caro mumbled, hugging her package.

"You know, I've been longing to meet you, Caro," Gram continued.

"Why?" Caro asked, frowning.

"Why not?" Gram replied. "Libby's told me a lot about you in her letters. You sound like a very interesting person." She looked at the package. "Don't you want to put that down? Or open it or something?"

"Yes . . . no! I mean, I'm going to put it down, but I don't want to open it, not right away."

Gram shrugged. "Suit yourself. You will anyway, won't you? Why don't you stow it under your bunk for the time being?"

"That's exactly what I intend to do," Caro said huffily, edging past Gram. She knelt and shoved the box under her bunk.

"By the way, what are you going to be for the Costume Parade on Sunday?" Gram asked. "I'm helping the rest of the Fillies with their costumes. I'd be more than glad to help with yours."

"Thanks, but I don't need any help," Caro said. "I can handle it by myself."

"Good for you!" Gram patted her on the shoulder. "I can't wait to see it." She reached up and took the witch's hat from the upper bunk. "Dru, here you go. Tomorrow you can paint it black. Matt has a spray can of black paint so all you'll have to do is give it a quick once-over. It'll dry in a jiffy. And Marie has an old mop that will make terrific long, stringy hair.''

"Gee, thanks, Gram!" Dru took the cardboard cone to which Gram had attached a wide cardboard brim and set it on her head. In a high, scratchy voice, she let out a witch-like cackle, and everybody broke up.

"As for your Indian costume, Danny," Gram said, "I'll show you how to fringe the hem of that mangy Ultrasuede rummage sale reject so it looks like a dress fit for an Indian princess. And, Libby, we'll turn that blue blouse of Marie's into a terrific jockey shirt. I'll take some darts in Pam's old tutu so it'll fit you to perfection, Penny. Lynda, I think that cider bottle helmet of yours needs a couple of feathers. I saw some ostrich plumes in the refrigerator box that would look terrific. We'll fasten them on with duct tape. Emily . . ." Her penetrating blue eyes narrowed just a little. "By tomorrow night, I have a very strong feeling that you'll know exactly what your costume's going to be. Yes, I'm sure of it."

Emily wished she was sure of it, too.

Chapter Seven

"Do you mean to tell me that your *grandmother* is going to coach us in volleyball and softball?" Nancy said the following evening as the Fillies and Thoros gathered up their bats and mitts after supper. "That's the nuttiest thing I ever heard!"

"That's because you don't know Gram," Libby said, grinning. "Come on, Nancy. Lighten up! Gram's not some old fuddy-duddy who sits in a rocking chair knitting socks. You've seen her around. She knows what she's doing, believe me."

"I'll believe it when I see it," Janet muttered, slinging a bat over her shoulder. "*If* I see it. This sounds pretty ridiculous to me. And the Long Branch boys will laugh themselves silly when they see her coming on the field."

"If they do, I'll beat 'em up!" Libby snapped. "Like Gram always says, where there's a will, there's a way.

And the Fillies *will* play better with Gram on our side, I just know it."

"Well, you certainly couldn't play worse," Ellen said.

"Wait and see. We're gonna be terrific," Libby promised.

But would they? Emily wondered just how much magic Libby's grandmother could create. It was going to take something pretty special to turn this group into anything even remotely resembling a team!

When the Fillies and the Thoros reached the softball field, they found Gram there waiting for them. She was wearing Libby's baseball cap, and she greeted them all with a big smile.

"What kept you, slowpokes?" she asked. "We don't have much time—have to make hay while the sun shines, you know, and it's going to set in about an hour. All right, young ladies, before we begin, I have some news for you. I've talked to Matt and Marie, and they've agreed to forget about the volleyball game on Field Day."

The Fillies cheered, and the Thoros groaned. Gram silenced them with an upraised hand. "Fact is, we just don't have time to practice that as well, so we're going to concentrate on whipping the Webster's softball team into shape. Now this is the way I see it. I've been watching all of you today riding and swimming, and I'm impressed. But you're used to doing things as individuals, not as members of a team. Hey, don't get me wrong—I don't expect you to turn into robots the

81

minute you pick up a bat and ball. Don't care much for robots myself—efficient, but boring. So this is what we're going to do. We're going to divide all you bright, pretty, intelligent, athletic girls into two teams, and then we're going to play ball."

Emily was really disappointed, and a little embarrassed for Gram. She'd expected the old lady to come up with some super strategy, but all Gram had suggested was exactly what they'd done before.

Libby voiced Emily's thoughts. "Uh . . . Gram, we've tried that and it didn't work. When the Fillies played the Thoros the other night, it was a disaster."

"Who said anything about the Fillies playing the Thoros?" Gram said, hands on hips. "I said we'd divide up into two teams, that's all. We'll call them . . . the Bays and the Roans! Okay, let's go. Lynda, you're the pitcher for the Bays, and Nancy, you pitch for the Roans. Libby, you're the Roans' catcher. Lisa, Bays' catcher. Emily, third base for the Bays. Beth, first base for the Roans . . .".

By the time Gram had finished assigning positions, each team was a mixture of Fillies and Thoros, though the Roans had one more Filly since there were seven Fillies and only six Thoros.

"Wait a minute!" Nancy said. "This isn't fair. I mean, I know you're the coach, Mrs. . . . uh, Gram, but now instead of one good team and one crummy one, we've got *two* crummy ones!"

"Depends on how you look at it," Gram said cheerfully. "The way *I* look at it, since you'll all be playing on the same team on Sunday, you have to get used to working together, helping each other."

"But we've got *Caro* in the outfield!" Nancy wailed.

Gram beamed. "Aren't you lucky? The Bays don't have an outfielder at all. Okay—Bays in the field, Roans at bat." She established the batting order. As the players took their places, she turned Libby's cap around so the visor was sticking out the back, and shouted, "Play ball!"

As the game progressed, the players began to attract an audience. Melinda and Warren strolled, hand in hand, over to the ballfield, followed by the Foals. Then Pam, Chris, Matt, and Marie joined them. Everyone cheered as loudly for the Bays as for the Roans whenever someone made a hit, and when Janet's double brought Lynda sliding home a split second before the ball landed in Libby's mitt, the spectators went wild. So did the Bays, Fillies and Thoros alike.

"It's all tied up!" Ellen shouted happily, pounding Lynda on the back. "Two to two! Way to go, team!"

"This is really exciting," Dru said happily as Emily stepped up to bat.

It was exciting, all right, Emily thought. She just hoped she wouldn't foul up—or out!

"Just relax, Emily," Gram said. "Keep your eye on the ball, and when you hit it, run like crazy!"

"*If* I hit it, you mean," Emily said with a rueful grin.

"Think positive," Gram told her, stepping out of

83

range of her bat. "Just do the best you can. Nobody can ask for more than that."

Nancy wound up for the pitch, then released the ball. Emily swung and missed.

"Stee-rike one!" Gram hollered as the ball thudded into Libby's mitt.

"Rats!" Emily mumbled. She missed the second pitch, too. The next three were wide and outside.

"Ball three!" Gram shouted.

Through narrowed eyes, Emily watched as the next pitch arced toward her, and swung with all her might. To her astonishment, she connected, and the ball sailed straight for the outfield. She sprinted for first base while Janet headed for third. Caro lunged forward, mitt outstretched, going for the catch—and made it. She stared down at the ball as if she couldn't believe her eyes, then looked around wildly. "What do I do now?" she cried.

"Nothing! That's the third out! Great catch, Caro!" Nancy shouted, throwing her glove in the air.

"Yeah, Caro—fantastic," Meghan added as the Roans trotted off the field and the Bays ran on.

Caro's face was flushed with pleasure and pride. "Sorry, Emily," she called over her shoulder. "That was a really good hit."

Emily laughed. "Thanks! And you made a terrific catch!" It would have been nice if she could have brought Janet home, but she didn't really mind. Nancy was slapping Caro on the back, grinning from ear to ear, as Beth gave her a "high five." It looked as if the feud between the Fillies and the Thoros was over at last.

"Where's Gram?" Emily asked Libby a little while later. The game had been called on account of darkness at the end of the fifth inning, with the Roans ahead, four to two. Now all the girls were gathered around the campfire, toasting marshmallows and making s'mores. The Fillies and Thoros were sitting together, and the Foals had just put on some skits they'd made up with Melinda's help.

"I'm not sure," Libby replied. She examined her marshmallow in the flickering firelight and, deciding it was done, plopped it on top of the chocolate bar and graham cracker Nancy was holding out. "She said she had to talk to Marie about something."

"Maybe she decided to go to bed early," Ellen suggested. "She must be pretty tired after the day she's had. My grandma takes a nap every day, and all she does is putter around her garden and go to Women's Club meetings."

Lynda snorted with laughter. "Gram? Tired? She's got more energy than all of us put together!"

"She's something else, all right," Caro said with genuine admiration.

"Hey, Dru, want s'more s'mores?" Janet asked. "I've just made another one, and I don't think I have room for it."

Dru hesitated, then shook her head. "No, I better

85

not. I want to lose another pound by Sunday. Gram says she knows I can do it if I just put my mind to it."

Libby grinned. "Gram thinks anybody can do *anything* if they just put their mind to it!"

Suddenly, Marie appeared in the circle of light cast by the fire, looking very solemn. She clapped her hands to get everyone's attention, then announced, "Foals, Fillies, and Thoros, it is my pleasure and privilege to inform you that, tonight, Webster's Country Horse Camp has been honored by a visit from a very special person."

"Hear, hear!" Matt called out, grinning.

"Who do you suppose it is?" Emily whispered to Danny.

"I can't wait to find out!" Danny whispered back.

"Ladies . . . and gentlemen," Marie added, nodding to Matt, Warren, and Chris, "please welcome that celebrated mind-reader, mystic, and medium, *Madame Beatrice!*"

Everybody whistled, cheered, and clapped as a wiry little gypsy stepped out of the shadows. She was dressed in a bright yellow blouse and a red print skirt with a long fringed sash of purple and blue around her waist. A red and white bandanna was tied around her head, and gold hoop earrings dangled from her ears. She wore lots of gold bracelets on both arms, and in her hands she held a crystal ball. Emily immediately recognized the gypsy's clothes—she'd seen them in Marie's refrigerator box. She also recognized the gypsy.

86

"It's Gram!" Libby shouted delightedly.

"So that's why she asked if she could borrow one of those big round light bulbs from the ceiling fixture in the kitchen," Pam said, laughing and pointing at the crystal ball.

The gypsy drew herself up to her full five feet two inches, and shot a mock-ferocious glare at Libby and Pam. In a thick accent that sounded very gypsyish to Emily, she said, "Who is zis Gram? Vhat is zis light bulb? I am Madame Beatrice, mind reader and fortune teller! I tell you ze past, ze present, and ze future. You do not beliefe me? Zen I show you!" She struck a dramatic pose and peered intently at the light bulb. "Ze past! Yesterday vas Toosday! Ze present! Today is Vensday! Ze future! Tomorrow is *Terzday!*" She made an elaborate bow as the campers laughed and applauded. *"Now* you beliefe me, yes?"

"Yes!" everybody shouted in chorus.

"I tell fortunes now. Here—" She thrust the "crystal ball" at Chris, who took it, grinning. "Ze visions I see are very cloudy. I sink crystal ball burned out! From now on, I read palms. Who vants to go first?"

"Me!"

"No, me!"

"I want to go first!"

The Foals surrounded the gypsy, eagerly sticking out their hands. She motioned for all but one of the little girls to sit down, and took the child's hand, bending over it with great concentration.

"Ahhh," she said in a stage whisper. "I tell you your

88

past, little one. About twenty minutes ago, you eat s'more. About five minutes ago, you also eat s'more. Now your future. If you eat one more s'more, you vill have *beeg* tummyache!"

The little girl giggled, and the rest of the Foals crowded around the gypsy again, but she continued looking into the palm she held. Smiling, she said, "You have keeten at home. You love heem very much. Hees name . . . hees name ees . . . Fluffy?"

The girl's eyes grew wide as saucers. "How did you guess?"

"Madame Beatrice does not guess—she *knows*," the gypsy said, patting her on the head and turning to the next child.

"How *did* she guess?" Penny whispered to Libby.

Libby shrugged. "Search me. I've never been able to figure out how she does it."

"I bet I know," Caro said. "I bet Marie let her look at all the campers' applications. Remember how we had to write something about ourselves? I'm sure that's it. Besides, palms don't show you things like that. I read a book about it once."

"Pipe down, Caro," Lynda whispered. "I want to hear. I can't wait till it's my turn. She read my palm last year, and told me I was going to win a blue ribbon. I thought she meant in one of our horse shows, and when I didn't, I was disappointed. But then Bluebell won first prize in the Four-H show, and I'll never doubt Gram again."

Emily privately thought that was stretching it a little,

but she was fascinated anyway. Caro was right—Gram was definitely something else!

When the last Foal's palm had been read, Melinda led her little group off to bed, and it was the Fillies' and Thoros' turn to have their fortunes told. They clustered around the gypsy as eagerly as the Foals had done, watching and listening in fascination while she studied hand after hand, telling each girl something about herself and her future.

"It's really spooky," Meghan said after she'd had her turn. "How could she know that my brother's name is Steve, and that my favorite color is blue?"

"How'd she know how scared I used to be of horses, and how much I love Donna now?" Dru wondered aloud.

"How could she possibly know that *National Velvet* is my very favorite book?" Danny asked.

Caro sighed impatiently. "Like I said before, Marie probably showed her the camp records, and besides, Libby's been writing to her, telling her all about us. There's nothing spooky about it."

"Libby, it's your turn," Lynda said, giving Libby a little shove.

But Libby just smiled and shook her head. "Nope. No point in it. Whenever the gypsy reads my palm, she always says . . ."

The gypsy reached out and touched her cheek very gently. "She alvays says, 'You haf made two old peoples very, very happy. That iss your past. I see in your

90

future that you will keep on making them very happy—and very proud.' "

"My turn!" Caro said, shoving her hand under the gypsy's nose.

The gypsy took her hand and looked at it for a long time, smoothing the palm with one finger. At last she said, "I see . . . I see that you are not vhat you seem to be. You haf a secret, a beeg secret. And I see that you vill be sad for a while, but then you vill be happy."

Caro snatched her hand away. She looked upset.

"That's just plain silly! You didn't really tell me anything at all!"

"Vould you haf beliefed me if I had?" the gypsy asked with a smile. "But vhat I haf told you iss the truth." She turned to Emily. "Now you."

Her fingers felt cool and dry as she took Emily's hand and peered closely at the palm. "Ahhh . . . I see that you are about to find out vhat you vant most to know. And you vill discover a treasure—a treasure of pure gold!"

Emily stared at her. "A treasure? Pure gold?" That didn't make any sense at all. Probably the gypsy was getting tired. After all, she wasn't really a gypsy with mystical powers. She was just a nice old lady.

"I think it's time for one last song," Marie said, coming over to the gypsy and resting a hand on her shoulder. "Madame Beatrice needs her rest, and so do we. Tomorrow's going to be a busy day. Chris, you choose. What shall we sing?"

Chris Webster picked up his guitar and strummed a few chords, looking up at the starlit sky. "How about 'Clementine'?" he said at last. He began to play, and everyone started to sing:

In a cavern, in a canyon, excavating for a mine,
Dwelt a miner, forty-niner, and his daughter, Clementine.

Oh, my darlin', oh, my darlin', oh, my darlin' Clementine,
You are lost and gone forever, dreadful sorry, Clementine!

Light she was and like a fairy, and her shoes were number nine,
Herring boxes without topses sandals were for Clementine . . .

As they launched into the chorus, an image began to form in Emily's mind. A miner . . . panning for gold. A golden treasure . . . his daughter, Clementine . . . Joker, the golden horse . . .

Suddenly Emily leaped to her feet. "I got it! I got it!" she shouted.

Chris stopped playing, and everybody stared at Emily as if she'd lost her mind.

"*What* have you got, Emily?" Marie asked.

"My costume! I know what I'm going to be for the Costume Parade!" she cried happily.

The gypsy nodded and smiled. "I told you you would," she said.

Chapter Eight

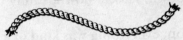

The next three days all ran together as far as Emily was concerned. She hardly had time to drop a post-card to her family and one to Judy—there wasn't a single minute to sit down and write a real letter. She'd have a lot of catching up to do next week when Field Day was over.

The very first thing she did the next morning after making her usual visit to Joker was to dash to the Activity Room and tip over the refrigerator box to see what was left for her costume. There wasn't very much, but Emily found exactly what she needed.

"Good thing I didn't decide to be anything fancy, like a princess or a queen," she said to herself as she hauled out a pair of brown corduroy pants with a hole in one knee (Chris's, she guessed), a badly worn plaid shirt, a vest that had obviously once been part of a three-piece suit, and a battered slouch hat. Then she dumped some odds and ends of trimmings and sewing equipment out of two shoe boxes and into an empty carton. They weren't herring boxes, but they'd do for Clementine's "sandals." As Emily raced back to the Fillies' cabin, she was whistling the song under her breath. She knew she'd look ridiculous, but that was okay. If she was grungy, Joker would look even more magnificent than he already was, and that was the most important thing. Maybe there wasn't an award for "Most Beautiful Horse," but if there was, Joker would win it hands down. *Hooves* down, Emily thought, and grinned.

From then on, everything was kind of a blur. Horse-manship classes, swimming and canoeing, softball practice, farm chores, and preparing the camp for Field Day came one after the other. All the campers, the counselors, Matt and Marie, Warren, Chris, and Gram were working at top speed, and Emily loved every minute of it. Libby's grandmother seemed to be everywhere at once, helping any Filly, Thoro, or Foal who needed it with her costume, lending a hand in the kitchen where Marie and Barbara were cooking up all sorts of delicious food for the Field Day barbecue, coaching the softball team (they decided to call them-selves the Bayroans), and never, ever seeming tired or irritable.

Chris and Warren fastened red, blue, and yellow pennants to tall poles around the Advanced riding ring, where the horsemanship competitions and mounted games would be held, and strung electric

94

Japanese lanterns in the picnic pavilion and through the trees of the grove where the barbecue would take place.

On Saturday, Matt handed out fliers to every camper listing the order of events on Field Day. Caro looked at hers and frowned.

"Why are the riding competitions first?" she asked Pam. "That means we have to change out of our riding clothes after mounted games, put on our swimsuits, change for softball, then put on our costumes for the parade. There won't be *nearly* enough time between the softball game and the Costume Parade for me to blow-dry my hair after my shower."

"Hey, what can I tell you?" Pam said with a shrug. "That's the way it's always been, and it always works out all right. Forget the shower, by the way—there definitely won't be time for that."

"No shower?" Caro cried. "But my hair will be an absolute *mess,* and I'll be *dirty!*"

Pam sighed. "Caro, plan on a quick sponge bath, okay?"

"When are you going to tell us what your costume will be?" Penny asked. "Is it going to be funny, or far out, or scary, or . . ."

"My costume is going to be *the best,* that's what," Caro said. "And as I keep telling everybody, it's going to be a surprise, so please stop asking me about it."

Gram, who had been listening without saying anything, said, "Are you sure you don't need any help with that costume, Caro?"

95

"No, Gram, I do *not* need any help," Caro replied with a toss of her head. "And by the way, are you ever going to tell me what you meant by what you told me Wednesday night at campfire? It didn't make any sense at all."

Gram's bright blue eyes widened innocently. "What *I* told you? Why, Caro, I wasn't even there. The gypsy told you whatever it is you're worried about. You'd better ask her what she meant—if you can find her, that is."

"Oh, forget it!" Caro flounced off.

"Gram, you're *terrible!*" Libby said, giggling. "Why are you teasing Caro like that?"

Her grandmother looked at her solemnly. "I wasn't teasing her, honey. I was just giving her one last chance to save herself from being very embarrassed tomorrow, and the poor child didn't take it. But live and learn, I always say." Then she brightened, smiling at the rest of the Fillies. "Seems to me it's just about time for us to go down to the vegetable garden and pick some greens for that salad Barbara's making for supper. And Marie needs lots of tomatoes for tomorrow, so we better be on our way."

What did Gram mean by saying Caro was going to be embarrassed tomorrow, Emily wondered, as she followed the others out of the bunkhouse. If she were Caro, she decided, she'd pay attention to what the old lady said. Gram knew what she was talking about, no matter how far-fetched it seemed.

* * *

96

As soon as the campers had finished breakfast on Sunday morning, they ran even faster than usual to the stables to groom and saddle their mounts. The first event of Field Day was scheduled for nine-thirty that morning, and everybody wanted to be ready before the Long Branch boys arrived. Each girl, from the oldest Thoro to the youngest Foal, was every bit as well groomed as her mount, in snug-fitting breeches, glossy boots, and a freshly washed and ironed shirt. We look like a whole bunch of Caros, Emily thought with a grin as she led Joker out of the stable to the mounting block and swung into the saddle. And she was sure that there wouldn't be a single horse, either from Webster's or from Long Branch, that was as beautiful as her big palomino. Emily had polished both Joker and his tack until everything gleamed. Filled with excitement, she watched the procession of cars, vans, and pickup trucks bouncing down the dirt road to the area that Warren and Chris had roped off for parking.

"I didn't realize there would be so many spectators," she said to Libby, who had come up beside her on Foxy. "Where are they all coming from?"

"Oh, from Winnepac and some of the other farms," Libby told her. "There's always a notice about Field Day in the *Winnepac Dispatch,* and there's not much to do around here, so everybody turns out to watch. And then there are some of the campers' families—mostly the Foals' and the youngest Long Branch boys' folks."

"I wish my family could have come," Emily said,

"but they couldn't get away this weekend. They're going to try to come next week, though."

"Hey, you've got Gram. She's everybody's grand-mother, remember?" Libby said cheerfully. "Look, here come the Long Branch boys!"

Emily looked where Libby was pointing. Sure enough, she saw horses and riders approaching from the direction of the Winnepac River. She tightened her grip on Joker's reins. Field Day was about to begin!

Since Emily's class was the second event scheduled, she and the other intermediate and advanced riders were able to watch the Beginners go through their paces. From their horses' backs, they had an excellent view over the heads of the spectators who lined the white rail fence surrounding the ring. When Dru won fourth prize in Beginning Horsemanship, all the Fillies whooped and cheered. Dru was grinning from ear to ear as Matt fastened the white rosette to Donna's bri-dle, then reached up to shake her hand.

Next came Intermediate Horsemanship. Emily took a deep breath and clucked softly to Joker, falling in line behind a tall boy on a rangy pinto. She turned and called over her shoulder to Penny, "Good luck!"

"You, too," Penny called back. Danny and Meghan waved as they waited to go into the ring.

Emily was surprised at herself—she didn't feel nerv-ous at all, in spite of the spectators and the four Long Branch boys who were entered in the event. She trusted Joker completely, and she remembered Gram telling her, "Just do the best you can. Nobody can ask for more than that." Well, she'd certainly do her best, and Joker would, too.

When the class was over, Emily was pleased that Meghan had won the blue. But when Matt held up a bright red rosette and called her name, she just sat there, staring at him. Surely he must have made a mistake—the skinny boy on the chestnut mare was a much better rider than she was!

"Emily, what are you waiting for?" Danny said, laughing. "If you don't want your ribbon, I'll take it!"

Blushing, Emily rode forward. She still couldn't quite believe it even when the Long Branch riding instructor, who was one of the judges, pinned the ribbon to Joker's browband and congratulated her. Her very first real horse show, and she'd won second place! Wait till she told Judy!

The last event of the morning was the Advanced Jumping competition, and as Chris and Warren set up the jumps, Emily dismounted and led Joker to a nearby grove of trees, where she tethered him in the shade. Then she threw her arms around his neck and gave him a big hug.

"Thanks, Joker," she murmured. "On any other horse, I probably wouldn't have won anything at all!"

"C'mon, Emily, let's watch," Penny called. She, Dru, and Danny were already on their way back to the ring, and Emily hurried to catch up. They managed to work their way through the crowd to the top row of bleachers just as Libby was beginning the course on Foxy, her light bay gelding. She completed the round with only three faults. One by one, the other riders took their turns, and after a final jump-off between Caro on Dark Victory and a Long Branch rider on a long-legged sorrel, Caro was declared the winner with a perfect round. Everyone cheered and applauded as the beautiful blond girl rode to the center of the ring to accept the blue ribbon, and the Fillies all yelled and clapped even harder when Libby and Lynda placed third and fifth.

Emily was so proud of her bunkmates, she thought she'd burst. And when Pam waved and grinned from the other side of the ring, Emily knew she was proud and happy, too.

During the picnic that followed under the tall shade trees behind the farmhouse, Long Branch boys mingled with Webster's girls as they ate sandwiches and salads and drank cold lemonade. Emily, Danny, Penny, and Dru felt a little shy and awkward, but Libby and Lynda met some boys they knew from previous years, and Caro was happy as a clam, surrounded by eager admirers. She could hardly tear herself away when it was time for the afternoon activities, beginning with Mounted Games, most of which Webster's won as Pam had predicted.

But Long Branch came into its own during the swimming and boating competitions. Webster's didn't stand a chance against the boys' superior strength,

speed, and skill, even though Nancy, who was a powerful swimmer, came in second in the butterfly race.

"Pam should have let you wear one of your bikinis," Lynda teased Caro when the girls were changing out of their swimsuits into shorts and shirts for the softball game. "You would have distracted the boys so much that they'd have forgotten how to swim!"

"Probably," Caro agreed smugly. "But that would hardly have been fair."

Emily caught Libby's eye, and they both smothered an explosion of giggles. Caro's good opinion of herself seemed to be growing by leaps and bounds, and it had never been particularly small to begin with.

"Ready to go, team?" Gram asked, as she jogged into the cabin. "I just checked on the Thoros, and they're all set."

"Hey, Gram, I thought you said the Bayroans' uniform was going to be red T-shirts and white *shorts,*" Libby said, eyeing her grandmother's outfit. Gram was wearing a red T-shirt, all right, but she had on her old, reliable jeans.

"Shorts at my age? No way!" Gram said firmly. She gave a little tug to the visor of the blue baseball cap. "Let's be on our way. Don't want to keep those Long Branchers waiting."

"But my hair's still wet," Caro complained as she reluctantly followed the others out the door.

When the Fillies and Thoros were all assembled, Gram gave them all a big grin. "If you're expecting a fancy pep talk, you're going to be disappointed. All

I'm going to say is this: Keep your eye on the ball, keep your mind on the game, and remember, the important thing isn't whether you win or lose . . ."

" . . . it's how you play the game," everybody finished for her.

"Hmmm. Guess I must have given this advice once or twice before," she said with a twinkle in her blue eyes. "Oh, and one other thing—don't forget that you're all Bayroans, not Fillies and Thoros. You're a team. All for one, one for all, like the Three Musketeers. Got it?"

"Got it!" the Bayroans shouted.

"Look out, Long Branch! Here we come!" Libby cried.

Chapter Nine

"Well, at least they didn't totally pulverize us," Lynda said an hour and a half later. She looked down at Gram, who was kneeling at her feet, wrapping one of Lynda's legs in a length of heavy-duty aluminum foil. "Do you think we have enough of this stuff? If we don't, Marie has lots more."

"We have enough foil here to wrap up an elephant," Gram assured her. "And plenty of duct tape to hold the knight in shining armor together. No, they didn't pulverize you. As a matter of fact, I think you did pretty darn well. Nine to six is a perfectly respectable score. Now stand still, Lynda, or else I'm going to tape your legs together, and you'll never be able to ride your horse in the Costume Parade."

"The Bayroans were great," Libby said, buttoning her jockey shirt. "We even lasted seven full innings. Last year the guys got twelve runs in the first five in-

104

nings, so the game was called. Now *that* was humiliating!"

Emily slipped a length of rope through the belt loops of Chris's old corduroy pants and tied it in a knot at her waist, adding, "Nancy's homer with the bases loaded was unbelievable! Did you *see* the looks on the boys' faces when that ball sailed clear into the woods?"

"Did I ever!" Danny said. "They just stood there with their mouths hanging open." She examined her reflection in the mirror hanging over the bureau. "You know, Emily, you were right. With my hair in braids and this headband, I *do* look like an Indian."

"And Dru looks exactly like a witch," Penny said, fluffing the short tulle skirt of Pam's old tutu. With her fine blond hair brushed into a soft cloud around her face instead of being tightly braided as it usually was, and a sequined tiara on her head, Emily thought she looked absolutely beautiful, and said so.

Penny blushed. "Thanks, Emily. And you look . . . well, you look . . ." She started to laugh. "You look really silly!"

"That's the idea," Emily said, laughing too. Now that Danny had moved away from the mirror, she clumped over in her shoebox sandals and peered into the glass. "But I think I need just one finishing touch." She picked up Caro's eyebrow pencil and began rubbing it on one of her front teeth. Yes, that was the effect she had in mind. It made her look as if she was

105

missing a tooth. She turned around and grinned broadly.

The rest of the Fillies—all except Caro, who was still in the shower—dissolved into whoops of laughter.

Dru, hardly recognizable in Marie's old black dress and her mop wig under the pointed witch's hat Gram had made, cried, "Oh, Emily, that's hysterical! Would you mind if I blacked out one of my teeth, too?"

"Be my guest," Emily said, making a low, comic bow. "Or I guess I ought to say, be Caro's guest. It's her eyebrow pencil."

Dru hurried over to the bureau and began blacking out her tooth. When she was through, she stared at her reflection and said in an awed tone, "Gee! I even scare myself!"

Libby strode over to the bathroom door and yelled, "Hey, Caro, get a move on! You've been in there for *hours!*"

"I have not," came a muffled voice from inside. "I'll be out in a minute."

Gram, who had finally finished with Lynda's costume, stood up and surveyed the six girls before her. Folding her arms across her chest, she nodded and smiled. "If all you Fillies don't win first prize in every category—the scariest, the funniest, the most original, and whatever else there is—I will be mighty surprised." Then she narrowed her bright blue eyes, focusing on Emily. "There's only one thing more you need," she said.

106

"There is?" Emily couldn't think of anything that would make her Clementine costume more effective.

"Yep." Gram climbed up into the bunk over Caro's and came back down with a small paper bag in her hand. "You're a miner, forty-niner, right?"

Emily nodded.

"And the golden treasure you've found is your horse, Joker, right?"

Emily nodded again.

"Well, let's make Joker *look* like a golden treasure." Gram took a small spray can and several plastic containers of golden glitter out of the bag. "When you saddle him up, spray some of this glue on his rump and withers, and even on his mane and tail. Then sprinkle the sparkly stuff all over him. He'll shine like the sun!"

"Oh, Gram, that's a fantastic idea!" Emily exclaimed. Then she hesitated. What if the glitter and glue hurt her beloved horse, or made him sick?

"Don't worry," Gram said, as if she'd read Emily's mind. "It won't do Joker a bit of harm, and you can sponge it right off after the Costume Parade."

"I'll do it!" Emily decided. "I'll do it right now. Thanks, Gram."

"We'd all better get moving," Lynda said. "It's going to take me a while to get to the stable—I can't move very fast in all this foil." She picked up her cider bottle helmet and settled it squarely on her head. "How do I look?"

"You look wonderful," Dru said. "That's the best costume I ever saw in my whole life!"

"Yeah, it's pretty cool," Libby added. Then she came over and pretended to knock on Lynda's foil-covered chest. "How long do you think you'll stay fresh in that can?"

"Pretty long, but I'll never be as fresh as you," Lynda teased.

Gram looked out the window and said, "The Thoros are leaving now. My, Meghan makes a real spiffy cowgirl. And Janet's Martian is pretty special, too."

The bareback rider, the knight, the jockey, the witch, and the Indian trooped out of the cabin. While Emily took off Clementine's shoebox sandals and tucked the bag of glitter and glue into a pocket of her baggy pants, Gram rapped smartly on the bathroom door.

"Caro? You all right in there? Need any help?"

"No, thanks. I'm fine. You go ahead. I'll be ready in a sec," Caro called out.

Emily and Gram looked at each other and shrugged.

"I guess I better go," Emily said. "See you at the Costume Parade, Gram. You *are* going to watch, aren't you?"

"Wouldn't miss it for the world," Gram said, following Emily out of the cabin. "Now you hurry up. You'll need some extra time to gussy up that horse of yours."

Grinning, Emily dashed out the door. She decided to take a shortcut to the stables, and as she hurried across the grass she almost ran right into Chris, who was headed in the same direction. He stared at her for a minute, then, figuring out who she was, said, "Emily? Who're you supposed to be—a bag lady?"

Emily stopped in her tracks. "A *bag lady?* No! I'm Clementine, the miner's daughter—like in the song we sang the other night, remember?"

Chris examined her outfit critically. "Guess you didn't strike it rich yet, did you?"

"Yes, I did," Emily told him, with a frown, "and I'm going to get my treasure right now. Sorry—gotta run."

"Hey, don't get mad," Chris called after her.

"I'm not mad, I'm in a hurry," Emily shouted over her shoulder. But she couldn't help feeling annoyed. She didn't really look like a bag lady, did she? Well, no time to worry about that now.

When she reached the stable, Joker stretched his neck over the door of his stall, whickering softly in greeting. But when Emily tried to kiss his nose, he tossed his head and backed away uneasily.

"It's really me, Joker," she assured him as she let herself into the stall. "I know I look a little strange, but I'm still me, honest."

After she had stroked his neck and scratched his forelock, Joker seemed to realize that this scruffy-looking person was the same girl who had been riding him for the past several weeks. He danced around a little when she sprayed the glue on his rump, tail, withers, and mane, but he didn't object too much, and he didn't even notice when she sprinkled the glitter on him.

As Emily saddled and bridled him, she saw some of the other campers in their costumes leading their horses and ponies out of the stable. They all looked so wonderful that Emily suddenly got an idea. She hadn't been able to bring her camera with her during the other events, but there would be time to take pictures before the Costume Parade began.

"Be back in a minute, Joker," she said, slipping out of his stall.

"Where are you going, Emily?" Libby called as she ran out of the stable.

"To get my camera," Emily said. "I want to take pictures of all the Fillies."

She was halfway up the path to the cabin when she saw Caro coming down. Caro looked absolutely gorgeous in a bright red Spanish flamenco costume with a full ruffled skirt and ruffled sleeves. Her blond hair was fastened in a knot at the back of her neck, and a fringed silk shawl was draped around her shoulders. Emily was about to run up and tell her how beautiful she looked when Matt strode out from among the trees along the path, obviously on his way to the ring.

"How do you like my costume, Matt?" Caro asked, striking a flamenco pose.

Matt looked her up and down. "It's beautiful," he said. "Don't tell me you made it yourself."

Caro laughed. "Of course not! My parents bought

110

it for me in Spain last year. I asked our housekeeper to send it to me, and she did."

So that was what was in the big package Caro hid under her bunk, Emily thought. She waved at them both as she passed, and heard Matt saying gently but firmly, "Caro, I thought you understood the rules for the Costume Parade. The girls are supposed to create their own costumes. Ready-made ones aren't allowed."

Emily really didn't want to eavesdrop, but her feet seemed to slow their pace of their own accord.

"But I can't sew," Caro said. "I'm all thumbs when it comes to things like that. And I had this perfect dress—it's what the Spanish girls wear when they ride their horses in the fiesta!" She sounded close to tears.

"I'm sorry, Caro," Matt said. Glancing over her shoulder, Emily saw him shaking his head. "Rules are rules. I can't let you enter the competition. You may ride in the parade, but you'll have to step aside when the judging begins."

"But that's not fair!" Caro wailed. "I'm sure it's the very best costume of all! I *deserve* to win first prize!"

"I'm sorry," Matt said again. "It wouldn't be fair to the other girls if I let you enter. I'm sure you understand that."

Emily entered the bunkhouse and took her Polaroid camera from the little shelf over her bed. She felt very sorry for Caro, but she knew Matt was right. Everyone else had worked very hard on their costumes, and it *wouldn't* be fair if Caro were allowed to compete.

112

Suddenly the cabin door was flung open and Caro rushed inside. Her face was as red as her dress, and her big, beautiful eyes were filled with tears. She glared at Emily.

"You heard everything, didn't you?" she asked angrily. "And I bet you're glad I've been kicked out of the competition, aren't you?"

"No, I'm not glad, Caro," Emily said. She sincerely meant it. "But didn't you know you were supposed to make your costume?"

"I knew that if I did, it would be a mess," Caro snapped, flouncing over to her bunk and plopping down on it in a sea of red ruffles. "I would have looked *ridiculous!* And why should I even bother to try when I had a costume that was much better than everybody else's? It's a silly rule anyway!"

Emily felt very uncomfortable. She didn't know what else to say, and she had to get back to the stable—the Costume Parade was going to start any minute now. She wished she could say or do something to make Caro feel better, but she couldn't think of a single thing.

"It's not too late to find another costume," said a cheerful voice from the doorway. Both girls looked around to see Gram standing there. "One of the Foals is having trouble with her rabbit suit—it split right up the back, and Melinda and Marie are sewing her up. And some of the Long Branch boys took a canoe out on the river. They haven't come back yet, so Matt isn't going to start the parade for another fifteen minutes."

113

She stepped into the cabin, fixing Caro with her sparkling blue gaze. "I offered to help you several times before, Caro. Now I'm asking you again. Will you let me help you put together a costume?"

Caro brushed away tears of anger and humiliation. "How can you do that in fifteen minutes? There's nothing left in the refrigerator box," she said with a sniffle.

Emily knew it was true—she herself had taken the last items of clothing. But she also knew Gram well enough by now to be sure that the little old lady had something up her sleeve.

Gram walked over to Caro's bunk, brushed aside a cascade of ruffles, and knelt down, pulling out a brown paper shopping bag from underneath it.

"Remember the gypsy?" she said, grinning at Caro. "Madame Beatrice—knows all, tells all?"

Caro nodded.

"Well, she just happened to leave her gypsy costume behind when she took off for her next engagement," Gram said. "And it's only right that she did, since everything came from Marie's refrigerator box." Dumping the contents of the bag next to Caro, she went on, "Of course, you're quite a bit taller than the gypsy, but you're not very big around. I wouldn't be at all surprised if these odds and ends would fit you pretty well."

Caro picked up the bright yellow blouse and held it between a finger and thumb. "But they're *used,*" she said, wrinkling her nose. "I *hate* secondhand clothing."

"*Caro!*" Emily shouted. "Do you want to enter the competition or not?"

"Yes, Caro, don't look a gift horse in the mouth," Gram added. "Well, what do you say?"

Caro looked from Gram to Emily, then back at Gram. In a very small voice she said, "I say, thank you, Gram. I'd like very much to be a gypsy."

"Terrific!" Emily cried. "But before you take off your flamenco costume, let me take a picture, okay?"

Caro sprang to her feet, smoothing her ruffles and adjusting her shawl. She took the same pose she'd assumed when she was showing off her costume for Matt, and Emily pressed the button. While the picture developed, she helped Gram get Caro out of the red dress and into the skirt and blouse. Then Caro took over, winding the sash around her hips, putting on the gold jewelry, and tying the bandanna over her hair. When she had finished, Emily and Gram stepped back to admire the effect.

"Caro, you are a really dynamite gypsy," Emily said.

Caro glanced in the mirror. "I am, aren't I?" She picked up the photograph, which had now developed completely, and looked at it. "You know, I think I look even better as a gypsy than I did as a Spanish lady. Mind if I have some prints made?" she asked Emily. "And don't forget to take some pictures of me in my new costume."

Emily met Gram's eyes, and they both grinned.

"Run along now," Gram said, picking up Emily's camera. "I'll take pictures of everybody because Emily won't have time. Scoot!"

"We're scooting," Emily said. "C'mon, Caro. I'll help you saddle Vic, or we're going to be late."

Caro followed her out the door, then stopped and turned back. She threw her arms around Gram and gave her a big hug. "Thanks, Gram. And thank the gypsy for me, too!"

The late afternoon sun beat down on the ring but a breeze off the river cooled the afternoon as it made the pennants flutter. The Long Branch boys and the rest of the spectators climbed onto the bleachers or found places along the white rail fence to watch the grand finale of Field Day. Matt marched into the center of the ring and announced loudly, "Ladies and gentlemen, the Costume Parade!"

Emily, her shoeboxes taped over her boots, slouch hat on her head, gripped Joker with her knees because there was no way that Clementine's big feet would fit in the stirrups. Joker's coat glittered as though it were made of pure gold, and Emily's eyes were shining every bit as brightly. The first riders, all Foals, entered the ring on their mounts. The Fillies would come next.

"Emily! Emily, look here!"

She glanced down and saw Chris running toward her. He was holding something in his hand. When he reached her, he held it up.

"What's that?" Emily asked, puzzled.

"It's a pickaxe. We use it for chopping tree roots sometimes, but I thought it looked like the kind of tool a miner would use," Chris said. "Take it—it'll really make you look like a forty-niner instead of a bag lady."

Laughing, Emily took it and slung it over her shoulder. "How's that?" she asked.

"Great. And Joker looks great, too," Chris said. "He's your treasure, right?"

"He sure is! Thanks, Chris," Emily said, and guided Joker into line behind Lynda. She looked over her shoulder, and saw Caro right behind her. Caro grinned at her and Emily grinned back.

"I tell you ze past," Caro called out. "Yesterday vas Saturday. I tell you ze present—today iss Sunday. I tell you ze future—tomorrow iss Monday!"

"I tell you ze truth," Emily shouted. "You are *nuts!*"

Caro giggled. "You know something? You are *right!*"

As the campers circled the ring, they made a very colorful display indeed. Everybody clapped, and the Long Branch boys whistled and cheered. Matt and Marie were standing in the center next to a man and woman Emily had never seen before—probably the judges, she decided. Pam had said one judge would be the art teacher from Winnepac High, and the other was the owner of Betsy's Boutique, where Caro loved to shop. Matt did a double take when he saw the gypsy. Then a broad smile spread over his face. Emily was sure she knew exactly what he was thinking—Libby's grandmother had done it again!

Another face caught her eye. It was Rachel, sitting in the bleachers with Pam, Warren, and Melinda. She was laughing and clapping harder than anyone, and she looked like her old, healthy self. The Thoros waved and grinned at her as they rode past, happy to see their counselor again.

Where is Gram? Emily wondered. Then she saw her climbing the fence. A tall, gray-haired man was helping her up. He steadied her as she perched on the top rail, then handed her Emily's camera.

"Hey, Grampa!" Libby shouted. "You made it! Hooray!"

Her grandfather blew her a kiss as she trotted by on Foxy, and Gram quickly snapped a picture.

Suddenly the air was filled with the sound of a brass band blaring a march at top volume. Emily looked around to see where the music was coming from, and saw Chris on the highest row of the bleachers, fiddling with the controls of a big tape player on the bench beside him.

"Better late than never," his father said with a grin. Cupping his hands around his mouth like a megaphone, he called out, "*Now* the Costume Parade has officially begun!"

As though inspired by the stirring music, the horses and ponies pricked up their ears, tossed their heads, and switched their tails, prancing around the ring while the judges scribbled in their notebooks and put their heads together. When at last they had made their decisions, they handed their notebooks to Matt, and

Marie waved at Chris, who turned off the tape in the middle of "The Stars and Stripes Forever."

The riders slowed their horses to a stop, and Emily bent down and patted Joker's neck. "I may look like a bag lady with a pickaxe," she said softly, "but *you* look magnificent. You just *have* to win a prize!"

Matt began announcing the winners in the various categories, and the proud campers rode over to accept their ribbons. The Foal in the rabbit suit won "Most Original"—she had fastened rabbit ears and a big white fluffy tail on her fat white pony to match her own costume. Lynda won "Most Elaborate," Dru won "Scariest," Beth, who was dressed as a ballerina, won "Prettiest," and Janet, the Martian, won "Most Spaced-Out."

As ribbon after ribbon was awarded, Emily's heart sank. And by the time all but the last one had been given out, she knew she and Joker hadn't won anything at all. She didn't mind so much for herself, but she minded a lot for Joker.

"And now for the final award," Matt said loudly, holding up a big purple rosette. "It gives me great pleasure to present the Grand Prize ribbon to the girl whose costume the judges have decided is the most creative and the cleverest of all—Emily Jordan, the forty-niner, and her solid gold horse, Joker!"

Emily's eyes got as round as saucers. "Me? Us? Joker and me?" she gasped as everybody cheered and applauded. It was really true! She'd won the Grand Prize for Joker, just as he deserved! The big palomino

119

arched his neck and pawed the ground as Matt pinned the rosette to his bridle and smiled up at Emily.

"Oh, thank you! Thank you so much," Emily said happily. Then she looked over at Gram, who was grinning from ear to ear. "And thank *you*, Gram," she called out. "Thanks for everything!"

"The Stars and Stripes Forever" started playing again, and as the riders made one last circuit of the ring, Caro came up beside Emily, matching Vic's pace to Joker's.

"It really is a good costume, Emily," she said. "Congratulations." Then, after a slight pause, "Uh . . . Emily, I'd just as soon nobody else knew about my other costume. I know Gram and Matt won't say anything, but . . ."

"I won't tell," Emily said. "I promise."

"Not even Libby?"

Emily shook her head solemnly. "Not even Libby."

Caro smiled. "Thanks, Emily. You're a pal."

As they rode out the gate and headed for the stables, Caro said, "Emily . . . I know this sounds silly, but . . . well, do you think Gram really *can* read people's palms and tell them what their future is going to be? Or is she just a very good guesser?"

Emily shrugged. "I don't know about Gram, but the gypsy seemed pretty good at it."

"She sure was." Caro smoothed the full skirt of her costume. "I think I'll keep this on for the barbecue. Who knows—maybe some of the gypsy's magic will

rub off on me. I met this really cute boy at the picnic, and I'd just *love* to read his palm!"

She urged Vic into a trot and rode off, bracelets tinkling. Emily followed more slowly, gazing at the purple ribbon that fluttered merrily from Joker's bridle.

"You're my golden treasure, all right," she told him softly, "and I don't need a fortune teller to predict that I'll love you forever and ever!"

When Emily's mom, dad, and brother visit her at camp, they bring along a wonderful surprise— her best friend Judy! Emily worries that Judy might be uncomfortable among Emily's new friends, but Judy fits right in. So why is Emily suddenly feeling so left out? And what is going on between beautiful Caro Lescaux and Emily's big brother, Eric? Emily is in for more surprises than she ever imagined before the weekend is over!

Don't miss HORSE CRAZY #4:
Surprise, Surprise!
by Virginia Vail

Virginia Vail is a pseudonym for the author of over a dozen young-adult novels, most recently the ANIMAL INN series. She is the mother of two grown children, both of whom are animal lovers, and lives in Forest Hills, New York with one fat gray cat. Many years ago, Virginia Vail fell in love with a beautiful palomino named Joker. She always wanted to put him in a book. Now she has.